PARTHUR

The Story of an Orphaned Bobcat

Dawn Fritz Hopkins

Saguaro Books, LLC
SB
Arizona

Copyright © 2019 Dawn Fritz Hopkins

Printed in the United States of America
All Rights Reserved

This book is a work of fiction. No part of this book may be used or reproduced by any means, graphic, electronic, or mechanical, including photocopying, recording, taping or by any information storage retrieval system without the written permission of the publisher except in the case of brief quotations embodied in articles and reviews.

Reviewers may quote passages for use in periodicals, newspapers, or broadcasts provided credit is given to *Parthur; the Story of an Orphaned Bobcat* by Dawn Fritz Hopkins and Saguaro Books, LLC.

Saguaro Books, LLC
16845 E. Avenue of the Fountains, Ste. 325
Fountain Hills, AZ 85268
www.saguarobooks.com

ISBN: 9781698367729
Library of Congress Cataloging Number
LCCN: 2019951349
Printed in the United States of America
First Edition

DEDICATION

This story is dedicated to the memory of my father, Kenneth Wilfred Fritz, who taught me to love and respect all things of nature.

Parthur and Dawn**

Author's Note

While this story happened during the early 1960's, and Parthur was a real and loving companion, the reader must be warned that these events could probably never happen again. Wild animals are not meant to be house pets. The reader should also realize there are facilities and professionals who provide assistance to distressed wild animals. This book is not intended to influence anyone to ever get close to a bobcat.

Parthur

Chapter 1

It was a small noise, but it was enough to make the young, inexperienced, mother bobcat stiffen with apprehension as adrenaline pumped through her body, heightening her sense of fear. She sprang silently to her large, padded feet and lifted her head, sniffing the air in search of the origin of that tiny sound that had alerted her. Her head slowly moved back and forth as her large ears swiveled, trying to home in on what had startled her. Her sudden movement had knocked aside the small, four-week-old, spotted kitten that had been nursing at her side. He lay sprawled at her feet with a dazed and sleepy expression on his face. The mother bobcat quickly lowered her head and gave the small kitten a nudge with her nose, but almost immediately she raised her head once again and nervously scanned the area in front of her. The kitten, unaware of any danger, raised itself on unsteady legs and leaned into the front legs of his mother. Once again, the mother bobcat anxiously leaned down and quickly sniffed her small offspring. She closed her eyes as she took in his smell.

She stepped over him and assumed a low, defensive crouch keeping her body on top of his. She looked steadily in the direction where she thought the sound had come. Her body was taunt, and the fur around the back of her neck and shoulders rose in fear and aggression. All four legs were ready to spring. Her back-left foot tapped soundlessly in apprehension on the rock where she stood, and a low growl rumbled from her throat. The baby understood this growl, and now he too was afraid and flattened his body to the rock ledge and pushed himself up against his mother's back legs–looking for security.

The two cats were motionless as they waited on their rocky ledge. Their tawny striped and spotted furs blended almost perfectly with the rocks and boulders strewn around them. The mother bobcat had been lured out of her den by a gloriously warm, sunny, fall afternoon with her first offspring. It was his first introduction to the great wide world outside of their den. But now something was terribly wrong. There was danger out there, and she didn't know what or where it was. She had to protect her little one and was frozen in fear.

Parthur

The bobcat kitten had been confused by his mother's quick and sudden movements. But once she had growled, he instinctively knew that something was wrong. His small pink tongue was still curled in the nursing mode and was just visible between his half-opened lips. Droplets of milk dampened the fur around his mouth, and the top of his head was still wet from the cleaning his mother had been giving him with her warm, sandpaper tongue. His gray-blue eyes were alert now as he crouched under his concerned mother. He could feel the tightness of her body, and her fear was transferred to him.

It was a warm, lazy, sunny afternoon in the foothills of the Maricopa Mountains in southwestern Arizona. A light breeze danced among the short, mesquite trees and cat's claw that made a thick ring below the ledge where the two bobcats waited. In among the trees' gnarled roots, the bleached dry, golden grasses waved back and forth with a soft crackle in the light breeze. The October sun hung low on the western horizon, washing the sky in a golden glow. Only a few elongated clouds hugged the horizon of the fall sky, and they were painted almost a crimson red from the fading sun. The huge gray and tan boulders that stood behind the cats' ledge were bathed in a warm yellow wash. Summer was stubbornly clinging to these rugged, rocky mountains.

The mother bobcat made another low growl, and the baby pushed up even closer to his mother's hind legs, folding his own legs under his chest so that he was now a small ball. He tried to be as still as he possibly could, and he closed his eyes and waited.

Hopkins

The small baby thought back in his memories. He had been born in a small, dark cave made up of smooth rocks that had been piled there centuries ago. After his eyes had opened and they had focused, he had been aware of the bright light that came in from the small, jagged entrance of that cave. His mother would leave every day to hunt, and while she was gone, he would curl up and sleep to await her return. But as he grew bigger and stronger, his curiosity of what lay outside his small den became irresistible. Several times in recent days he had poked his head out the small hole and looked in wonder at the things around him. He knew he was not to venture outside his home, but he loved these quick looks into the world outside.

Today had been different, however. He had been asleep when his mother entered the cave, but once she was next to him, she sat down and started to clean his face. He was instantly awake. He could smell the blood that was caught in the fur around her mouth from the rabbit she had eaten prior to her return. He licked her face and mouth clean and relished in the taste of it. Then his mother stood up and walked to the entrance of the cave. She stopped halfway there and called to him, urging him to leave the cave. She walked out the small hole, stopped and turned and called once more. The little kitten did not need much coaxing, he was anxious to see what was out there. He moved as quickly as he could on slightly, unsteady legs out of the dark cave to join his mother.

The setting sun hit him straight in the face, so it took a few moments for his sight to adjust. His small round eyes were not focusing completely, yet, to see in the distance, but he could see well enough to delight in the smallest of things. His first encounter was a large, black beetle that was moving slowly across the rock ledge in front of their den. The small kitten stopped and stared at the slow-moving black bug. He patted at it several times and then tried to shove it with his right paw. The beetle pulled in its legs and played dead. It didn't move, in hopes that the kitten would tire of its game and spare its life. For several minutes the small kitten batted at it and pushed it one way and then another.

His mother, sprawled on the rock ledge nearby, watched him indulgently. But the warm sun on the kitten's back was just too appealing, and his stomach told him that he wanted to nurse. He abruptly left the large beetle to make its escape and walked over to his mother to nuzzle her belly, looking for a nipple. He flopped down next to her. She gave a half turn of her body to help in his search, looked at him with pleasure, and then she laid her head down on the rock ledge once he had found an engorged nipple. Her front paws flexed open and shut ever so slightly.

His small mouth nursed eagerly, and small droplets of milk spilled out on either side, wetting his face. His eyes were closed in contentment, and his front two paws kneaded her soft belly around the nipple. He felt secure and happy as the late afternoon sun caressed his back. The rock ledge on which he and his mother lay was warm, having soaked up the rays from the sun all day. He could not have known, however, that his late-summer birth meant danger for his survival. Most baby bobcats are born in the spring, but his mother's estrus, by some quirk of nature, did not happen until midsummer. The chances of this baby making it through the winter months would be doubtful. He might not be strong enough or big enough by the time winter entered these mountains that he called home.

Now everything was topsy-turvy. Fear had gripped this little family. The mother bobcat growled again. She raised her body from her crouch and lifted her nose high into the air one more time with eyes squinting and whiskers twitching. Her nostrils quivered as she tried to find a smell that would tell her what it was that had frightened her. The small tufts of fur on the ends of her ears flickered forward and backward as they swiveled, looking for something, anything. A light breeze rose from the trees below her and ruffled the fur on her back, but her body stayed almost motionless with her baby curled beneath her feet. She lowered her head and searched the distant area.

Everything had gone completely silent on their mountain ledge. Seconds before, the air had been filled with the normal sounds of a late fall afternoon in the low mountains, but now no insects buzzed, no birds chirped and no animals scurried. There was just a deadly silence, as if every living thing in the area was holding its breath, knowing that danger was nearby. The little bobcat's mother knew without a doubt that something was out there, somewhere, and she was exposing her new cub to whatever it was. She waited motionlessly. Nothing moved on her body except her short, striped tail which flicked anxiously back and forth as she listened intently. Once again, she cautiously raised her head to sniff the air in hopes of finding the meaning or the direction of the threat, and her eyes closed again as she rapidly inhaled great gulps of breath looking for clues in the air. She sensed nothing.

The silence was suddenly broken by a sharp, explosive report that cracked through the dry air. The mother bobcat was slammed in her chest and fatally wounded by the deadly accurate shot from a hunter's rifle. Her body was savagely thrust back from where she had been standing by the impact of the bullet. Her legs felt weak as she staggered to keep her balance. She could see her small, frightened baby just in front of her, but her vision was quickly dimming. Panicked, she tried to understand what had happened.

Blood was seeping from a mortal wound, but with a mighty effort she staggered forward, put her nose down to her cringing, kitten's face and breathed in his smell one last time with a shallow, ragged breath. Small droplets of blood oozed from her nose and soiled the fur on the top of his head. She closed her eyes and collapsed on top of him as that final breath left her body. Her last thoughts were to protect him from whatever it was that was out there. Her body went slack as it covered her most cherished possession, and her life left her limp body.

The baby bobcat was terrified. What had happened? What was wrong with his mother and why was she not moving? He mewed softly to her, hoping to get an answer. There was only silence. She did not move or make a sound. Her weight on top of him was heavy and uncomfortable. He laid there for a few minutes, hoping she would move, but when she didn't, he decided to try and get his legs up under his body so that he could stand or possibly crawl out from under her. Over and over he tried to move, but the dead weight of his mother on top of him was just too much. He was trapped. He felt something wet on his back. It was his mother's blood seeping from the gunshot wound. It matted into his fur.

Even though he was almost paralyzed with fright, every instinct in his young mind told him he had to flee, but he knew that wouldn't work because he couldn't get his legs and body loose from under his mother. But why should he run; this was his mother? She had always meant warmth, food and safety to him. Things must be all right, because she was here. But things were not all right. His mother's body was silent, deathly still and very heavy. Finally, the little bobcat decided not to struggle any more. He would stay put and just wait. He tried to curl up as best he could under the dead weight of his mother, and he waited.

Ten minutes went by, and it felt like an eternity to the small baby as it lay in fear. Then he heard it. It was far away, and then it got closer and closer. He curled up in fear into an even tighter small ball under his dead mother and closed his eyes.

The two hunters, dressed in blue jeans, sweatshirts, denim jackets and well-worn cowboy hats were making their way slowly over the rocky and uneven terrain just below the den of the baby bobcat and his mother. One of the men, the shorter of the two, was doing most of the talking. The other hunter, a tall, thin, serious-looking young man, only replied to his companion with short, quick replies. The conversation of the shorter hunter only stopped when he had to exert himself as he traversed a particularly large rock or ditch, and then he would continue. Adding to the sounds of the human voices that the young bobcat heard were the thumping and scraping noises made by their heavy, hiking boots as pebbles, rocks and dirt gave way or were crushed under their heavy soles as they approached. The dry sage brush scraped and rasped against the legs of their jeans, and the low limbs of the mesquite trees and the cat's claw grabbed at their jackets. The baby bobcat listened in fear and confusion as they got closer and closer. And then he knew that they had made it just below his ledge.

Suddenly, all the noise stopped. The small kitten opened his eyes and listened intently. Maybe whatever it was had gone. But then the strange noises started all over again. He closed his eyes tightly, and with a cold dread in his stomach he listened to the strange sounds of the two humans talking just below the rock ledge where he lay hidden under his mother's body.

The hunters were young men in their early twenties, and they were being very careful in approaching their kill, or at least the tall one was. He wanted to be certain that the bobcat he had just shot was dead and not just wounded. A wounded bobcat can be quite dangerous, and he didn't want to take any chances. The two young men had stopped their progress just below the little rock ledge that held the sprawled body of the mother bobcat and her hidden baby for several minutes. Her still body was just visible from their vantage point, and the taller hunter watched the downed animal carefully, looking for any sign of movement. Finally, the tall hunter pulled himself tentatively up on the ledge, keeping his rife ready.

When on the small ledge, he knelt in a crouch four feet away from the cat's lifeless body. Again, he watched for any movement. Finally, certain the animal was dead, he stood up and carefully approached its lifeless body, carrying his rifle loosely in his right hand. He lowered his rifle and carefully nudged the bobcat's body with its barrel. Then he slowly kneeled by its side, placing one knee on the rock surface and steadying himself with the butt of his gun. He saw the bloody wound of his rifle shot in the cat's chest and was satisfied that it was dead.

"Jack, that was a heck of a clean shot," the shorter hunter said from below the ledge. He could just barely see up on the rocky platform, but he had watched his friend's careful approach to the dead animal. "You got that one clean as a whistle."

"Yeah, Mike," Jack grunted as he remained squatted at the head of the dead mother bobcat. He had soft gray eyes, and upon close examination one could see the admiration he felt for the animal he had just killed. Jack Copeland and his good friend, Mike Summers, had decided to go bounty hunting that afternoon. It was the fall of 1960, and the state of Arizona was still offering bounties on animals such as bobcats, coyotes and mountain lions that were considered threats to the livestock of the local farmers in the area. Jack liked to hunt and used hunting as a way to bring food to the dinner table. This kill was for bounty and pelt money, which he needed for his family. He had a great respect for the wildlife of Arizona-bobcats in particular. They were beautiful and graceful animals. He felt some regret in taking this animal's life. He shook his head slightly and gave a tug at the front of his cowboy hat as he surveyed his kill. "Can't be thinking that way, not now," he thought.

Jack reached over and carefully propped his rifle up against a large rock next to the dead body of the bobcat and reached into his jacket pocket and took out a pair of heavy canvas gloves. Slowly he put them on as he stood up. "Let's get this one back to the trucks before it gets dark. It's going to get chilly here as soon as the sun goes down behind those mountains." Jack nodded towards the western skyline. The sun had slid below the horizon, and golden rays were now streaking over the darkening, crimson sky. A purple hue painted the far mountains with the loss of the sun for one more day.

Jack grabbed the front paws of the dead bobcat with both hands and started to swing its body up onto his shoulder for transport back to his truck. But as he started to lift the lifeless body into the air, he stopped in surprise as he uncovered the small baby. Jack stood there frozen for a moment with the limp body of the mother bobcat dangling from his gloved hands. He then placed her carefully to the side as he looked down at the shivering, terrified animal.

"Mike, look at this."

Mike couldn't see what Jack was staring at, but he quickly leaned his rifle against a small tree, hurriedly climbed over a few rocks and pulled himself up on the small ledge next to Jack. He looked down in amazement at the small, blood-smeared body of the frightened baby bobcat.

The small, infant animal had kept its eyes tightly squeezed shut, but now that the weight of his mother had been removed, he decided to take a peek. He looked up at the two giant men in front of him and was terrified. He looked quickly from side to side to see if there was some escape route or a place to hide. The edge of the ledge was to his left, that wasn't any good. The taller man was to his right, and he was in between the small kitten and the hole to his den. He closed his eyes in fear again. The two men started talking, and he was certain that one of them was getting even closer.

He opened his eyes once more to look, and he was horrified to see one of them lean down to get a closer look at him. The small kitten backed up a few inches and hissed and slapped one of his front paws on the ground in the direction of the tall man near him. His little ears were flat against his head.

"Damn, I never would have shot its mother if I had known she had young. It really is unusual that she would have a cub this late in the fall." Jack studied the small animal in front of him. "I'll bet he isn't any more than four or maybe five weeks old." Jack was feeling a little guilty now about his kill. He had unknowingly made an orphan of this little bobcat, and he didn't like the feeling. "Damn," he muttered softly under his breath. "Damn."

Parthur

"What are you going to do with it, Jack?" Mike asked. "The state gives us a bounty on a bobcat, no matter its age. Are you going to kill it?"

Jack felt sick in his gut as he looked down at the miserable kitten. It looked so small and vulnerable. Jack had killed its mother, and its only chance to survive. He knew in his heart that he couldn't harm this small, defenseless animal, but he also knew that it was way too young to make it on its own. But he wasn't quite sure what he could do for it. Jack shifted his weight several times as he stared in silence at the little animal in front of him and hesitated.

"Jack?" Mike asked again. "Are you going to kill it?"

Jack rubbed his chin in deep thought, and then he slowly untied the dusty red bandana from around his neck. He removed his battered old, black cowboy hat and wiped the inside of the head band with the red cloth as he continued to study the frightened animal.

There was another long silence. "Jack?" Mike questioned his friend again.

"No," Jack mumbled softly.

"What did you say, Jack?"

"No," a little louder this time. "No, I can't do that." He resolutely placed his cowboy hat back on his head, placed the bandana in his back jeans pocket and stood up as he took off his over-sized, denim jacket. Once the jacket was off, he laid it on a nearby rock. He found the two zipper ends and zipped up the jacket halfway. Then he made a knot in the bottom of the garment. It became obvious to Mike that he was making a carrying pack.

Mike watched him in surprise. "What are you doing, Jack? You aren't really thinking about taking that kitten back with us, are you?" When Jack didn't respond, Mike continued, "What will Nancy say?"

"Look, I killed its mother, and I feel responsible. I'll figure out something to do with the baby when I get back. I'll handle Nancy." Jack didn't want to appear to be soft in front of his hunting buddy, but he just couldn't kill this defenseless animal. When he had shot the mother, it had only meant money to him. But now the dead mother had left him this legacy, and he couldn't back away from the responsibility. Jack didn't want to meet the questioning eyes of Mike as he finished preparing his jacket to carry the kitten, and he hurriedly finished the job. He had made up his mind, and that was that.

Fortunately, Mike didn't pursue the matter any further. He stood there in silence as he watched Jack. In fact, if the truth were known, Mike was relieved that the baby was going to be saved.

Jack didn't have a clue what he could do with a small baby bobcat. He and his wife, Nancy, were living in a cramped, old, dilapidated trailer on the outskirts of Gila Bend, Arizona. She had been his high school sweetheart, and they had married just after graduation three years ago. She was a waitress at a local truck stop in Gila Bend, but Jack had recently been laid off from his construction job on U.S. 80. There was a lot of love, but not a lot of money in the Copeland household. Jack knew he couldn't murder this little, defenseless kitten for the bounty just because there were problems in his life.

As Jack worked on the carrying sack, Mike kept an eye on the small kitten. The baby bobcat backed slowly into a small depression in the rock wall and tried to curl up as tight as it could, facing the two men. Mike didn't interfere with the kitten's retreat; there really wasn't anywhere the little guy could go.

Trembling with fear, it watched the two humans. The men's voices were so foreign to its ears, and every time they moved the small kitten pushed harder and harder against the stone wall. A couple of times he hissed at them. Things were just too confusing.

When the carrying pouch was finished, Jack tentatively reached over with his gloved hand and paused just above the kitten's head. The small animal reacted in terror as it hissed and spat at the large glove. Then Jack grabbed the back scruff of the baby's neck as tenderly as possible and lifted the small, frightened animal into the air. The little bobcat writhed and turned as it was lifted, and it batted ineffectively with its small paws at the big gloved hand that was holding him. Jack carefully placed the small, struggling animal into his makeshift jacket-sack. He zipped the zipper to the top, being careful not to catch the fur of the little animal. He folded over the open end of the jacket on to itself, crisscrossed the empty arms to secure the opening and then lifted up the bundle by the arms of the jacket to his shoulder. The baby bobcat was secure. He gently adjusted the small sack on his shoulder till it felt comfortable, leaned over, picked up his gun and stood up.

"Mike, you carry the mother's body. We had better make tracks back to the trucks. It's getting late, and that sun went down fast."

The two hunters turned south for the two-mile hike back to their vehicles. Jack was deep in thought about the responsibility he was carrying on his shoulder. He knew that his wife loved wildlife as he did, but he wasn't certain what she would think about a wild, baby bobcat as a member of their family. How could they keep him? To say they didn't have much room was an understatement. The two-room trailer they shared was old and small. A pet was a luxury Jack and Nancy had never considered. Could a person really make a pet out of a wild animal? Jack didn't have an answer for that one, but his real concern was the expense of feeding another mouth. Granted, it was a small mouth now, but what would happen when it became a full-grown bobcat? A full-grown bobcat, now that was a thought. How do you cope with a full-grown bobcat? He knew that he and Nancy really couldn't afford this addition to their household right now. He had no job. The questions kept rolling over and over in his head as he and Mike slowly made their way back to their trucks.

Mike, usually a big conversationalist, didn't say much on the return trip to their vehicles. However, he couldn't stop himself from glancing over periodically at the small bundle hanging over Jack's left shoulder as they walked back to their trucks, but the extra weight of the dead bobcat mother on his shoulder made him concentrate on his own path as he picked his way over the low, mountain terrain.

Jack felt the little kitten squirm a few times when they first started off, especially as he struggled and slipped over several large boulders. The kitten mewed pitifully for its mother as it was bumped and tossed about in the dark carrying sack on Jack's shoulder. It squirmed and fought against the denim material of Jack's jacket as it looked for an escape. But after about a half-hour the little bundle was very quiet and still.

Jack made a silent promise to himself and to that small, scared baby. He would find an answer somehow.

Parthur

Chapter 2

It took Jack and Mike almost two hours to hike back to their trucks through the low, mountainous, rocky terrain. As they approached their vehicles, the sky was almost a pitch black. Luckily, a three-quarter moon had risen over the north mountains, so they were able to find their way easily. A chill had quickly moved into the valley with the absence of the sun's warmth, but the strenuous hike over uneven terrain had kept both men warm on their return trip. When they arrived, Mike hoisted the body of the mother bobcat into the back of his truck. "No need to upset the little baby with her smell," he said.

Jack nodded.

Hopkins

"I'll take care of the bounty with the state authorities and I'll get the pelt to that guy on Harper Road. I think you've got your hands full." Mike jumped into the front seat of his truck. He slammed the door and rolled down the window. After two tries, the engine caught. Mike turned on his head lights, shifted the truck into first gear and waved goodbye out of the opened window to his friend. His battered, black, '56 Ford bumped down the deeply, guttered dirt lane and was out of sight around a sharp bend just a couple hundred feet down the road.

Jack stood there in a cloud of soft dust raised by the truck's tires and watched the two red rear lights disappear. The baby bobcat was still hanging over his back in his jacket as he watched the black truck drive out of sight. Suddenly, he felt a slight movement on his shoulder.

At that moment Jack remembered all the blood that had been on the kitten. "I wonder if you're hurt?" he said out loud. Carefully, he carried the bundle to the passenger side door of his truck. Balancing the kitten-bundle in one hand, he opened the door and laid it carefully on the front bench seat. The overhead light in his truck was dim. He had taken off his gloves for the hike back to the trucks, but now he removed them from his back pocket and slid them back on his hands.

He unzipped the jacket as slowly as he could to be certain that he didn't catch any part of the small animal inside. Finally, the tiny bobcat was exposed. The kitten looked up at Jack with fear and then burrowed into one of the sleeve openings of the jacket. He didn't get far. Jack reached in with his gloved hand and lifted the baby with his hand under the animal's stomach. He pushed the jacket out of the way and sat him down on the car's front seat. The little kitten stood stiffly on all four legs with his ears flattened to his head. Jack ran his gloved fingers down each leg, around its neck and back, and then he picked him up and turned him over so he could inspect his stomach.

The little bobcat trembled in fear as the big hand moved over its body, but the little animal gave no resistance to the inspection. His only response was to hiss at Jack periodically. Jack could not find any injuries on the small kitten. He was satisfied that the matted blood in the kitten's fur was from the gunshot wound to its mother. Jack pulled his jacket over and re-arranged it so that he could replace the kitten back into the make-shift pouch. He carefully re-zipped the bundle.

"Well, little one, we've got to get you home." Jack stood there for a minute in the open door of his truck looking down at the round bulge in his blue denim jacket on the front seat. There was no movement. He closed the passenger door softly which made the over-head light go out. Jack made his way around the back of his truck in the dark to the driver's door, opened it and slid in. The inside light was back on and he looked at the bundle for any sign of movement. There was none. He sighed deeply as he took off his canvas gloves and put them on the seat next to the bundle. He closed the driver's side door as softly as possible. He leaned back against the backside of the seat and fished the keys to his truck from his front jean pocket. When he found the ignition key among all the rest of his keys, he pushed it into the ignition keyhole and started the engine. The engine caught on the first try. He hesitated for just a moment and then put on his head lights, put the truck into gear and started down the dirt road that led to the interstate.

It was an hour and a half drive back to Jack's trailer outside Gila Bend. He talked off and on to the small concealed animal next to him in soothing tones in hopes that his voice would give some reassurance of safety to the kitten. Jack watched as best he could while driving, but he was certain that the little bobcat never moved once on the whole trip back to his home.

The small kitten did listen to that low, soft voice but he was so frightened he didn't know what to think. The voice did sound nice though, and it didn't sound like it would hurt him. He hadn't liked the inspection that Jack had given him before they left, but the big man hadn't hurt him. The sound of the truck's engine and the car and truck noises outside Jack's vehicle paralyzed the small animal with fear. Where was his mother? He didn't feel safe. All he wanted was to cuddle up to her warm body. He felt lost and miserable, and he was starting to get hungry.

When Jack finally drove into the small trailer park where he and Nancy shared their old, white trailer, it was almost 10 o'clock. It was almost pitch-black outside, since the moon was high in the late autumn sky. There were fifteen trailers in the small neighborhood, all nestled under a grove of large cottonwood trees. Lights were visible from several of the other trailers, and Jack could see that Nancy was back from her job at the truck stop. Her car was pulled up by the front door of their trailer. The kitchen light cast a warm glow through the closed yellow curtains at the window that was positioned at the right end of the mobile home.

Jack pulled his truck up to the front door next to Nancy's car and turned off the engine. He sat there for a few moments in the driver's seat with both hands on the steering wheel in deep thought. *Am I doing the right thing?* he questioned himself again. Finally, he opened the door and looked over at the hidden baby bobcat in the denim bundle on the passenger seat. He started to retrieve his gloves and put them on, but then he thought better of it and laid them back down on the front seat. He opened the car door, leaned over and carefully, with both hands, picked up the jacket bundle. He awkwardly moved out of the front seat of his truck. He used his rear-end to knock the door closed.

Nancy had seen the lights of Jack's truck as he pulled up to their trailer. She had opened the front door and was standing there watching him, a little puzzled, as he gently carried the small bundle against his chest and walked toward her. "What do you have, Jack?"

"I'll explain inside." Jack squeezed by her as she held the door open for him. He carefully sat down on the faded blue couch that took up most of the area they called the living room of their trailer. Nancy closed the door, moved over to turn on a lamp next to the couch and stood in front of him. Her questioning eyes met his. His hands surrounded the bundle in his lap as he looked up at her.

"What is it?" she asked again. This time her voice was just a little tentative and had a touch of fear in it.

"I don't want to scare him anymore than he already is."

She was about to join him on the couch but thought better of it and moved a few steps backwards toward the door. "Him? What do you have in there?" Now she was a little scared.

Jack carefully unzipped and peeled back his jacket to expose the small animal inside. The bobcat kitten had been curled into a tight ball, but once it felt the material of the jacket released from its back, it lifted its face and peered up at the two of them.

"Jack, what is that?" Nancy moved a few steps closer now. She was certain that what she was looking at was some kind of cat or kitten, but she had never seen a feline that looked like the one in her husband's lap. It had a distinctive ruff of hair surrounding its small face with stripes radiating from its eyes. Its ears were huge and pointed with tufts of fur. She instinctively shied backwards again and lifted her hands defensively in surprise.

"It's all right," Jack calmly said.

Nancy relaxed a little but was still on guard.

"Come over here and sit by me so you can see him better." His voice was so reassuring, that she complied and moved away from the door and sat tentatively next to him. Both hands were in her lap, but she leaned toward Jack to get a better look.

Parthur

Jack touched the top of the baby's head with a soft stroke and then another and another. At first the little kitten struggled to get away from the big hand that was stroking its head, but Jack had placed his left hand firmly on its back and held it tightly in place on his lap. Jack persisted with his soft pats, and the kitten relaxed just a little. The big, foreign hand did not seem to be a threat; in fact, it felt good but where was his mother?

Jack continued with light strokes to the kitten's body, and he could feel some of the tension leave the small animal. While he held the kitten in his lap, with low soft tones he told Nancy about his hunt and what had happened to the baby's mother. When he finished the story, Jack and Nancy sat in silence for several minutes. Both were deep in thought about the situation.

Finally, Nancy said, "I'm glad you didn't hurt this little one." There was more silence. "I don't know what we can do for it but I know you did the right thing." She reached over and carefully touched the top of the little bobcat's head.

The kitten didn't shrink from her touch. In fact, he was starting to like the feel of their hands on his fur.

"When was the last time he had anything to eat?"

"Gosh, I don't know. It's probably been several hours for certain."

"Jack, he's a baby. He has to have food several times a day." Nancy jumped up from the couch and rushed into the small kitchen area of the trailer. She reached up into a cupboard and took out a saucer and filled it with a little milk from the refrigerator. She hurried back to the couch and placed the saucer on the floor.

Jack tentatively removed his jacket from around the small kitten. With both hands around the middle of the animal, he placed him on the floor of the trailer next to the saucer of milk. The kitten just stood there and looked up at the two of them sitting on the couch. Nancy leaned down and pushed the saucer directly in front of him.

He lowered his head and sniffed at the white liquid. He was hungry and could smell the milk, but he wasn't quite certain what to do with it. He stepped forward with his right paw, placing it right in the middle of the milk in the saucer. Milk spilled out onto the floor. Quickly he lifted his round, wet paw. Then he carefully tapped at the milk, spreading droplets of the cold liquid around the outside of the saucer. He retreated a few steps when it splashed up into his face. The kitten licked the few droplets of milk that had stuck to the fur around his mouth.

Jack reached down from the couch and gently pushed the small kitten forward to the saucer and plunged the tip of his face into the milk.

The small animal blew small milk bubbles out his nostrils. He lifted his head and licked his face again and liked the taste. His stomach was empty and this white stuff in front of him tasted good, almost like his mother's warm, sweet milk.

Jack pushed the kitten's face back to the saucer. Finally, the little baby got the idea and took a lick. Then he took another. It was cold, but it was good. In no time the saucer was empty. Nancy filled it once more before the baby seemed to have had enough.

"We have to give him something more substantial than milk." Nancy sat in thought for a moment on the couch and then said, "Wait a minute. That new couple next door, the Andersons, have a small kitten. I'll bet they have something he can eat. It's late—I hope they are still up."

Jack nodded.

Nancy jumped up and raced out the trailer door.

Jack remained seated on the couch, and the small animal looked up and eyed him carefully. He wasn't as frightened as he had been, and his empty stomach felt better. The kitten sat back on his haunches and began to clean himself. He licked his front, right paw and then whipped his face with it, cleaning off the milk residue. The little animal repeated the process several times as Jack watched.

Then Jack remembered the dried blood on the kitten's back and head. He jumped up from the couch and retrieved a small washcloth from the kitchen and damped it with warm water. He carefully lifted the small animal to his lap. The little kitten did not resist, and Jack washed off the blood from its fur.

Nancy was back in a few minutes, carrying a small can of cat food labeled 'tuna'. "The Andersons were just about ready to go to bed. Let's try some of this." She quickly found a can opener and removed the lid. Jack placed the small animal back on the floor, and Nancy then placed the small can in front of the little bobcat and sat dawn next to Jack on the couch to watch.

Hopkins

The little kitten sniffed the contents of the opened can once and twitched his whiskers. It had a strong, unfamiliar fishy odor. He sniffed it again and took a lick. It really didn't taste half bad at all.

Jack and Nancy watched as he ate half of the small can of cat food.

When he finished eating, the tiny bobcat looked up at the two of them. They hadn't hurt him, and they had given him food. They did seem so big, though. He slunk back toward the closed door of the trailer and called for his mother with soft mewing sounds. Things were so confusing in this new world. He wanted his mother.

Jack walked over and scooped up the animal and returned to the couch. He held him gently on his lap while stroking his head and body. The little animal did not resist his touch.

Nancy watched closely. "He is so darling." She reached over and gave him a little pat on his back. "But should we really keep him, Jack?" She hesitated as they both sat in deep thought. "He's so cute now, but he's going to grow up and be a big wild animal someday. Can we deal with that?"

"I know," Jack answered. Again, there was a long silence. "I feel so responsible for him. I killed his mother." They both sat there thinking about that. "Maybe we can find a zoo or something that would take him." Jack continued to stroke the back of the small animal. The kitten relaxed, closed its eyes and enjoyed the pleasure of his touch. "I'm going up to Phoenix next week for that job interview; maybe I could go by the Phoenix Zoo." Another pause. "I'll bet they would take him."

Parthur

"That's a great idea." Nancy brightened as she pondered the solution for the kitten. "It will be kind of fun taking care of him for a few days, though. He's so cuddly." She reached over and patted the bobcat's head again and scratched him behind his right ear. "Look, he really likes it when I scratch behind this ear," she said. The kitten pushed up against her hand to do it again. Nancy obliged.

Jack fixed a large cardboard box for the kitten that night and Nancy put in a soft terry towel at one end for him on which to curl up. The kitten burrowed under the towel immediately. He was exhausted. So many confusing things had happened but no one had hurt him. His tummy was full and he felt a little better now but he still missed his mom. He called for her one last time as he smuggled into the soft folds of the old blue towel and fell into a restless sleep.

Chapter 3

Four days later…

I pulled into the deserted parking lot of the high school. It was Saturday morning, and I checked my watch. It showed 5:20 in the morning. I was ten minutes early. I parked the big, sage green, nine-passenger Chevrolet station wagon in the middle of the empty student parking area. I yawned as I scanned the black asphalt area with its horizontal columns of white parking lines and looked toward the eastern horizon. There was just a hint of the approaching day as a sliver of light blue pushed out the dark of the night in the lower eastern skyline over the Maricopa Mountains of southern Arizona. None of the girls I was expecting to meet were there yet, so

I reached down and turned off the ignition and the headlights but I left the parking lights on. The brand-new station wagon belonged to Kofa High School and still had a hint of that new car smell in it.

A smile crossed my face as I thought about why I was there. I had grown up in Illinois but had graduated from the University of New Mexico this past spring. I had been a commercial art major and had secured a job with a local advertising agency in Albuquerque upon graduation. But the pay was deplorable. By the first of August, I knew I had better look for something else.

I had taken enough education classes at the University of New Mexico to qualify myself for a teaching job. I decided to see what teaching jobs were available in New Mexico or maybe in the surrounding states. When I walked into the placement office at the University and gave them my qualifications, they suggested I call Yuma, Arizona, about a teaching position they knew was available there. I didn't know much about the state of Arizona, and I had never been to the city of Yuma. But I took down the telephone number of the superintendent of schools in Yuma and called him as soon as I returned to my apartment.

"Hello. Dr. Robert Sirrine?"

"Yes."

"This is Dawn Fritz. I just graduated from the University of New Mexico this past spring with a Bachelor of Fine Arts Degree. I majored in fine arts and have a minor in anthropology and English. I understand that you might need an English or art teacher?"

The telephone interview started out well. I tried to present myself as capable, eager and personable. Yuma had just built a brand-new high school, Kofa High School, on the eastern edge of town, and the school board was having difficulty filling some of the last teaching positions for the faculty. In 1960, qualified teachers were hard to find, especially in Yuma, and the school would be opening its doors in just four weeks.

"So, you were an art major with minors in English and anthropology," said Dr. Sirrine. "Why anthropology?"

"The University of New Mexico has a great Anthro Department, and I really enjoyed those courses. In fact, I was on a dig with the University last summer in Santa Fe."

"That must have been interesting. What was the dig all about?"

"We were looking for the first capital of New Mexico founded by the Spanish explorer, Onate, before his group established Santa Fe."

"Did you find it?" asked Dr. Sirrine.

"We sure did." I went into a short explanation of the dig and some of our finds.

Dr. Sirrine quizzed me some more about some of my other classes in college and my interests. He must have liked what he was hearing. "And are you employed right now?"

"Yes, I am currently with a commercial art agency here in Albuquerque." There was a short pause in the conversation. I quickly added, "I know I could teach classes in either art or English." I had my fingers crossed that he would consider me for the job.

'Did you do any student teaching while at the University?'

'Yes, at Albuquerque High School. I did a class in English and one in art. I really enjoyed it."

The conversation continued for another ten minutes as Dr. Sirrine interviewed me. "Dawn, I think we might have a place for you here at Kofa High School. I will have to look over your college transcripts and I will need some personal, written recommendations."

"I can have all that sent to you this week."

"Great, if everything looks in order, I think we will be able to send you a contract."

"Oh, thank you, thank you, Dr. Sirrine, for giving me this chance," I gushed. "I'll do my best to prove to you that you made the right decision."

"I'm sure you will, Dawn. I will be in touch."

I was offered the teaching position at Kofa High School within two weeks.

When I arrived at my new job in September, I slipped easily and confidently into my assignments. I felt like I was a natural born teacher, and I loved my job and all my students. And my pupils really seemed to enjoy my classes. Maybe it was because I was young and approachable. Since Kofa High School was a brand-new high school, there wasn't even a senior class yet-just freshmen, sophomores and juniors.

I taught four English classes, all of them to juniors, two art classes and was the sponsor for the school yearbook. On top of that, I was going to direct the school play in spring. I had my hands full.

Now here I was, sitting in the school's station wagon in Kofa High School's parking lot waiting for four of my students to arrive on this early Saturday morning. I smiled again as I recalled how I had been talked into being their driver.

The previous Friday, as the bell rang for the end of the last period of the day, I was standing at my desk as my students were hurrying out the door to begin their weekend activities. "Goodbye, Miss Fritz. Have a nice weekend," a short, dark-haired girl remarked as she hurried past my desk.

"You, too, Maria."

It was Friday. They all wanted to forget about books and class work, it was the weekend. The doorway to my classroom was clogged as the pupils from my last English class for the day pushed their way to the exit. However, two girls were excitedly pushing their way through the exiting students into my classroom. "Miss Fritz. Miss Fritz." they exclaimed as they finally made it through the crowd of departing students. "We have a big favor to ask you." They stood breathlessly in front of my desk.

"Do I need to be sitting for this one?" I asked good-naturedly as I stood next to my chair.

"Well, maybe," Amy said with a giggle as she looked sideways at Beth. Amy Stanton and Beth Ryan were best friends and were students from one of my junior English classes. Both were good students with bubbly personalities.

"All right, girls, what can I do for you?" I sat down behind my desk, folded my hands on the desktop and looked up at the two girls.

"Well, both Beth and I are on the girls' golf team," Amy breathlessly began.

"Yes," I answered as Amy hesitated. "Go on."

"Well, the boys' golf coach does give us instruction, but we need a girls' golf coach."

"Amy, what has this got to do with me?"

"Will you be our golf coach?" Beth blurted out.

I was stunned. "Girls, I can't be your golf coach. I don't even play golf. The only golf I know I learned from one semester of golf from a physical education class at college."

"You really don't need to know how to play golf to be our coach," Amy answered. She looked shyly over at Beth and continued. "What we really need is a driver for our out-of-town meets." The two girls looked at each other a little sheepishly then back at me.

"Please, Miss Fritz. Will you do it?" Amy asked. "There are only four of us on the team, and you were everyone's first choice."

"Please? Please?" Beth pleaded.

So here I am, a week later, in the deserted school's parking lot waiting for "my" golf team. I laughed to myself at my new title of "golf coach." I'd gotten a 'C' in college for my one semester, effort at the game. I was certain my golf instructor from the University of New Mexico would have found my new title quite surprising. She had been generous in giving me that 'C'. My four-girl golf team from Kofa High School had their first meet in Phoenix.

Suddenly, the headlights of two more cars could be seen entering the empty school parking area. I got out of the school's station wagon, stood in front of the big car and waited while the cars drove towards me and parked.

Parthur

"Hi, Miss Fritz." Amy Stanton yelled as she and Beth jumped out of the back seat of her parents' car. The other two teammates exited the other car, carrying their large golf bags.

"Hi, girls." I quickly introduced myself to the sleepy-eyed, hastily dressed adults that were following their offspring as they all walked up to me. I quickly moved to the back of the station wagon and opened the rear door. Everyone helped in the arrangement of the golf equipment in the back. Once everything was in place, I closed the back hatch with a thud and turned to the parents. "It will be late when we return back to Yuma tonight since it is a double meet. I'll drive your daughters home when we get back. There is no need for you to be waiting for us here when we can't be too certain at what hour we shall return."

The parents all thanked me for being their daughter's driver as the four girls scrambled into the vehicle. Three of them piled into the back seat. Amy had moved a little slower. She hesitantly climbed into the passenger side front seat, a little shy being in the front seat with a teacher. I moved into the driver's seat, started the engine, and my golf team and I headed out of the school's parking lot. The parents all waved and yelled good wishes.

"Get all pars," one dad yelled.

"Get a birdie for me," another added.

It was a little past 5:30 in the morning. by the time we were on the road heading for Phoenix. The four-girl team included Amy and Beth, who had talked me into being their "coach," and Carol and Kathy who made up the rest of the group. I had Kathy in one of my English classes, but I did not know Carol as she was in one of the other junior English sections.

The four girls were all excited about the upcoming golf event. Of the four, Amy was by far the quietest, but she was able to hold her own as the conversations in the car went from golf, to school, and of course, to boys. Amy sat sideways in the front seat so that she would not be left out of the conversations in the back seat. I entered their chit-chat occasionally, but I knew their discussions were guarded. After all, a teacher was listening. The chatter was endless, however, as we headed out of Yuma driving straight east. The sky in front of us was turning from a dark blue to a pale yellow with the morning sunrise.

"We'll stop in Gila Bend for breakfast," I interjected.

Everyone agreed.

An hour and a half later, I pulled the big station wagon off the highway onto the frontage road in Gila Bend. I chose one of the larger truck stops and waited as a large truck backed out of a parking spot close to the front entrance. The five of us tumbled out of our vehicle. As we entered the front door, the smells of eggs, bacon, sausage and fresh brewed coffee greeted us as we looked for a place to sit down. The truck stop was almost full, but one of the waitresses, Nancy Copeland, waved us to the only empty booth that was just being cleaned up from its last occupants. The bus boy gave the table one last quick wipe as 'my' golf team and I eagerly sat down. Nancy gave each of us a menu. Everyone was starved.

Parthur

As we were all reading the bill of fare, Amy absent mindedly pushed the sleeves of her sweater up her arms exposing many small scratches all around her wrists. Beth was sitting next to her and looked over at the red wounds.

"Hey, Amy, what are all those marks on your arm?"

Everyone looked up from their menus as Amy pushed up the sleeves of her sweater even further and held out both of her arms for inspection.

"Our cat just had four kittens. They are about six-weeks-old now and do they ever play rough."

Nancy, the waitress, arrived at our table just as everyone was examining the tiny red scratches on Amy's arms.

"That's nothing," Nancy said. "You should see what we have."

Everyone at the table looked up at Nancy in expectation.

"What?" Beth asked.

"We've got a baby bobcat."

The group was hushed by the announcement.

"A bobcat. How did you ever end up with a pet bobcat?" I asked.

"Well, I'm not sure I would call it our pet," Nancy explained. "We've only had him for less than a week but my husband plans to take him to the Phoenix Zoo." She gave a short explanation of how they had ended up with the orphaned animal, and how they wanted to do right by it.

When Nancy finished her story, there was a moment of silence around our table as we all took in what she had told us. I had listened with rapt interest and wistfully said, "I have always wanted a bobcat as a pet."

The four girls now all turned and stared at me with shock.

"Miss Fritz, you aren't serious, are you? Beth asked in wonder.

"You really would want a wild animal as a pet?" Carol added.

"Yes, I really would." I looked into the faces of the four young questioning girls, and I thought back to my first encounter with a pet bobcat.

While at the University of New Mexico, I had taken many anthropology classes. My favorite teacher was the head of the department, Dr. Frank Hibben. He had a pet bobcat. On one occasion in my senior year, I and several other anthropology students had been invited to the professor's residence. As we entered the front door of Dr. Hibben's home, his adult pet bobcat took one look at the group and rushed behind a long couch in the living room. Everyone was amazed Dr. Hibben had a wild animal as a pet. He assured our group of students that the bobcat was quite harmless, and that it probably would not appear again. His bobcat hated strangers.

We were all there to inspect some ancient Indian pots that were going to be placed into the University's museum. They had been unearthed by a local rancher, and Dr. Hibben wanted to share their discovery with some of his senior students before they would be placed behind glass. As we all stood in his front entryway contemplating his unorthodox pet, he indicated that we should all move on down the hall to his den to see the pottery artifacts. Everyone started towards the den, but I hesitated. All the other students were eager to impress Dr. Hibben with scintillating conversations about Indian pots, their designs and carbon dating. But all I wanted to do was to make contact with his illusive pet. Forget about the pots.

As the group followed Dr. Hibben down the hall, I walked over to where his pet was lurking behind the couch and knelt on the floor at one end in hopes that I might make contact with him.

"He really doesn't like strangers." Dr. Hibben had obviously missed me in the den or had seen me make the detour. He had come back to the entryway and saw what I intended to do.

"That's all right. I'll just stay here for a few minutes to see if I can gain his trust. Is that alright?

Dr. Hibben thought about it, shrugged, and then turned and walked down the hallway to the rest of the students in his den. I could hear the murmur of their discussions but I decided to stay put. I sat down on the floor at the end of the couch. I was glad they had all left since I felt the loud talking might be scaring the animal.

I leaned back against the wall and slowly slid to the floor and looked down behind the coach. The cat was sitting on its haunches facing me, but just out of reach. It was dark behind the coach but I could see the yellow of his eyes as he stared hard at me. I stayed motionless for a good five minutes with my hands in my lap, and then I carefully moved one of my hands and slid it slowly across the floor behind the couch in his direction, palm up. He gave a little warning growl from deep in his throat, but he did not move away. I was not going to be deterred and I held my ground and spoke softly to the animal, urging him to come to me. Ever so carefully I pushed my hand in further and wiggled my fingers just a little bit.

Finally, my patience paid off. Bobcats are a curious breed of feline and, slowly but surely, the cautious animal moved just a little closer to my hand and those fascinating, wiggling fingers. He reached out his nose, sniffed them suspiciously and then immediately pulled back but, a few minutes, later he moved a little closer and sniffed again. This time he did not move away. Slowly, he moved even closer to my hand and took in its smell. Now, I was able to carefully reach out and gently pat his head. The cat stood his ground and allowed me to stroke him down his back. He stretched in pleasure. I moved away from the couch a bit, dragging my arm and hand with wiggling fingers moving ever so slowly. The cat followed those fingers as I pulled them slowly from behind the couch. He had just exited his hiding place as Dr. Hibben returned to the room.

"Well, I don't believe it. He really must like you. You are the only stranger I have ever seen who could get close to that cat."

The cat stared at Dr. Hibben and then looked back at me. I patted the cat's head one more time, and then he bounded away into another part of the home. The idea of having a pet bobcat was certainly implanted that evening.

Now here I was, with someone else who had one of those beautiful animals. Maybe this was my chance. The waitress had said they weren't going to keep the kitten. Maybe I could make my dream come true.

"You wouldn't consider giving the kitten to me, would you?"

The four-girl golf team stared at me in shocked silence. They couldn't believe what they had just heard their teacher ask.

"I mean it. If you are not going to keep it, would you consider giving it to me?"

Nancy was speechless for a moment. When this whole conversation had started, she had never considered the possibility that someone would actually ask to take the small bobcat. She looked at me and studied my face. She felt that I was certainly serious in my request. Maybe this was the answer she and Jack needed. The baby bobcat had accepted them as surrogate parents, but Nancy was just a little frightened of him. Even though Nancy had told me and the four girls they were going to give the animal to the Phoenix Zoo, she and Jack had never gotten around to making that call. Maybe the zoo wouldn't take the animal. What would they do then? And their trailer was so tiny. She and Jack really couldn't keep him. Without much more hesitation, Nancy looked at me, "Are you certain you would want him?"

"Without a doubt."

"Well, if you are sure."

"Absolutely." I added quickly.

"All right. He's yours, then," Nancy hesitantly said. She wasn't quite sure how she was going to tell Jack what she had just done but this young woman seemed so sincere. Nancy hoped she was doing the right thing. What would Jack think? This had all happened so quickly. Could she convince Jack they should give their small charge to this stranger? She looked again at the young woman seated in front of her. She seemed so nice and she obviously wanted to take on the responsibility.

"That's great" I shouted. I couldn't believe I had just adopted a baby bobcat. My mind was racing. I had so many questions. "Does he have a name?"

"No," Nancy replied. "No, we haven't named him, yet."

"Is the kitten male or female?"

"He's a male."

"What does he eat? How old is he?" The questions for Nancy came tumbling one after another.

Nancy answered them all as best she could. She had to leave our table several times to wait on her other customers but each time she returned I had more questions for her to answer.

The four girls ate their breakfasts in wide-eyed silence as they listened in disbelief to the conversation. All through the meal, Nancy and I exchanged information. It was decided I would pick up the baby bobcat on the trip back from the Phoenix golf match that night. Suddenly, I turned my attention to the four girls. In all of my excitement I hadn't taken them into consideration. "Is this going to be a problem for any of you? Do any of you have any strong reservations about sharing the car with a baby bobcat on our return trip home?" My mind was racing. I knew I was responsible for these four young girls but how dangerous could a four or five-week-old baby bobcat be? "I won't do this if any one of you has any anxieties about this." I looked closely into each girl's face.

The girls were speechless for a few seconds. They looked at each other then looked back at me. Each of them quickly agreed they could handle it.

"In fact," Amy said, "it sounds kind of exciting. "Just think, we will be in a car with a real live baby bobcat."

Oh, I hope I am doing the right thing, I thought. I couldn't believe what I had just done. I didn't have a clue how to raise a baby bobcat. Growing up in Illinois, my family had always had lots of cats and other animals around. *Certainly*, I rationalized; *this would be the same as raising a big cat and, because Nancy was quite certain it was only four or five weeks old, surely the five of us would be in no danger on the drive home. I shoved that thought out of my mind right away. My dad had always taught me to respect wildlife and he had always stressed wild animals should be returned to the wild. They are not meant to be pets but this one had lost its mother.* I wanted to do the right thing with this orphaned kitten.

Nancy gave me a pencil-drawn map to their trailer. I looked at it, asked a few questions about some of the turns and then tucked it into my purse as we got up to leave the restaurant. "We should be back about nine tonight," I told Nancy. I grabbed Nancy's hand as we were leaving and looked into her eyes, "Please know I will take good care of him."

Nancy nodded.

The five of us got up from the booth, paid our bills at the register and walked to the front door of the restaurant. The girls proceeded out to the car, but just before I exited, I turned back and caught Nancy's eye. I smiled and waved to her, and she waved back. I could tell there was some concern in her face. I tried to look as confident and responsible as I could as I walked out the door.

When we were back in the station wagon, the rest of the trip to Phoenix literally flew by. The conversation now was only about the new pet that was going to share the ride home with us.

"Can we give it a name, Miss Fritz?" Amy asked.

"Sure," I answered. "Let's see. Seems like it should have something to do with golf. We are on a golf trip."

"And the waitress said it was a male," Beth added. "Maybe 'Putter' or 'Arthur'."

"Something to do with par would be nice," Kathy giggled. "We certainly will be needing some of those later today."

"Parthur." I exclaimed. "Parthur would be perfect." And Parthur it was.

The girls were excited. I wasn't sure if all this commotion was going to hinder or help their golf games that day. I didn't think what I had just done was part of Golf 101. It surely made the two and a half-hour trip from Gila Bend to Phoenix go by in a flash. I knew I had made a rather hasty decision, but any doubts I might have had, I quickly dismissed. This was something I had dreamed about ever since that first encounter with Dr. Hibben's pet bobcat.

Chapter 4

When Nancy Copeland got home that night from her job at the truck stop, she opened the door of their small trailer to find her husband, Jack, sitting on the couch holding the bobcat kitten in his lap. The kitten's eyes were closed as Jack carefully stroked the animal's back. The small animal looked so peaceful and sweet. Nancy wasn't sure how she was going to tell Jack she had given the kitten away that morning to a complete stranger.

"Hi, Jack," she said as she closed the door to their small trailer.

"Hi, Nancy. Busy day?" He stopped what he was doing as he looked up and smiled at her. Then he quickly turned his attention back to the baby bobcat in his lap.

"No, it was pretty slow all day." She hesitated and then dropped her keys in a small bowl that sat on a table by the front door of the trailer. She closed the door of the trailer and let out a little sigh as she walked over and sat down next to Jack on the old couch. She watched as he stroked the small baby. The two of them sat in silence for several minutes. "It is amazing how he has accepted you, Jack. It's only been just a few days."

"Yeah, I know."

There was more silence.

How was Nancy going to tell Jack what she had done? "Jack, a young woman teacher from Yuma came in the restaurant this morning with four of her students on a school trip to Phoenix."

Jack nodded.

"Well, I told her about our kitten, and she became very interested."

More silence.

"Jack, I hope I did the right thing but I told her she could have him."

Jack had been half listening to Nancy, but now she had his attention. "You what?"

"Jack, she seemed so eager and was so convincing, I just felt it was the right thing to do."

"Nancy, I was going to call the Phoenix Zoo."

"I know but you haven't done it yet and maybe they won't take him. What will we do then?"

Both of them contemplated what Nancy had said.

"You know we can't keep him," Nancy added.

"Yeah, I know. But how do you know she can take care of him?" He was just a little irritated at his wife for making this decision about the kitten without talking it over with him.

"I don't," she shot back. "But wait until you meet her, Jack. She seems so kind and sincere."

"When is she coming for him?"

"Tonight."

"Tonight?"

"Yes, Jack, they are on some sort of school golf trip to Phoenix and will be by here around eight or nine."

Jack thought about what Nancy had just told him. He really didn't want to give up the small animal but he knew, in his heart, he and Nancy had no business keeping an animal such as this. He also knew Nancy was just a little frightened of the kitten. "I'm sorry, Nancy. I shouldn't have snapped at you. I'm sure you have done the right thing." He stroked the back of the little animal that was curled up in his lap once again. "It would have been nice if we could've kept him a little longer, though," he added, wistfully.

"I know, Jack." Nancy could tell Jack was certainly getting attached to this small bundle of fur. She also knew they had no business even thinking about raising this animal.

Chapter 5

It was almost seven that evening by the time the four girls and I left Phoenix. The golf team had been successful at their meet, winning three out of their four matches. Kathy was the only member of the team who had lost her match and was listening quietly as the other three girls chatted about how they had won their separate games. Amy suddenly realized they were leaving Kathy out of their conversations. "Kathy, you lost by only two strokes. You'll win next time."

Kathy was trying her best to be as enthusiastic as she could about the other girls' successes but losing by two strokes just wasn't a win. She had been ahead of her opponent all day up until the last two holes. She hit a fairway sand trap on both the seventeenth and eighteenth holes of her match. Her opponent had taken advantage of her bad luck. Kathy was not good in the sand. She felt as if she had let the team down in that she was the only loser of the group and she sighed.

As the station wagon left the city lights of Phoenix and its suburbs heading south, the conversations quickly switched from golf to the baby bobcat that was waiting to be picked up in Gila Bend.

"I can hardly wait to see him, Miss Fritz," Amy said. She was sitting in the front passenger seat of the station wagon again. "I'll bet he is really cute." She hesitated for just a bit and said, "Do you think he will be frightened of us?"

"I don't know, Amy, but he's certainly been through a lot in his short little life. We will have to be very gentle with him." My mind was racing. I hoped I was doing the right thing. Could I really handle a pet bobcat?

I pulled the station wagon off the highway into Gila Bend around nine-thirty. Everyone in the vehicle had become very quiet with anticipation. I removed the small pencil-drawn map Nancy, the waitress, had given me from my purse and referred to it using the light off the dashboard when we were on the back roads of Gila Bend.

Amy quietly slipped over the back of the front seat and joined the other three girls in the back. "I'll sit back here, Miss Harper, and give Parthur the front seat," she said. To be honest, she felt just a little more secure in the back seat of the large station wagon with the rest of the girls, even if they were a little squished.

Parthur

I had to pull the station wagon over to the side of the road twice and turn on the inside lights to refer to Nancy's map as I tried to find our way to the Copelands' small trailer in the dark night. Once I made a wrong turn but made a quick U-turn to get us back on track but now the large vehicle was bumping down a small gravel lane that led to a cotton-wood grove where I could see a group of trailers huddled under the trees. A lone light pole with a dim light shining downward cast a soft yellow glow on the road ahead of me. As I drove, using my left hand only, I glanced once more at the map in my right hand to be certain I knew which trailer was the right one. I pulled up to the front of a small and old, white mobile home. Beside it were two vehicles; an old truck and a well-used, rusted white car.

I turned off the engine of the station wagon but left the head lights on. I turned and faced the eager and excited faces of the girls in the back seat. "Let me ask you one more time. Is anyone afraid?"

All four girls shook their heads "no".

"Can everyone handle this?"

This time all four heads bobbed up and down in the affirmative in silence.

"We all have to remain calm and quiet," I continued. "He'll probably be scared. Do you all understand this?"

Again, there were affirmative nods from the back seat.

I took a deep breath as I turned and looked out the windshield at the weather-beaten trailer awash with the lights from the station wagon. "Surely they wouldn't be in any danger," I thought to myself. It is only a kitten but it is a wild kitten. I resolutely opened the station wagon door and walked up to the front door of the trailer.

Nancy opened the trailer door before I could knock. She had seen the lights of our car as we drove in. "We were starting to get worried about you. Did you have trouble finding us?"

"Yes, just a little but your map was pretty helpful." I stood awkwardly on the steps leading up to the doorway.

"Come on in, come in," Nancy quickly said as she stepped out of my way and waved for me to enter the trailer. Jack had been sitting on the couch as I crossed into the small living room. He stood up as I entered, "This is my husband, Jack. Jack this is Dawn Fritz."

He stuck out his hand and I shook it. His handshake was strong, and I liked what I saw in his eyes. There was gentleness there, in spite of his rugged good looks. I hadn't been certain I was going to like someone who had killed a baby bobcat's mother. Nancy stood next to him, and he draped his arm over her shoulder. The three of us exchanged pleasantries for a few minutes. He and Nancy seemed to be a nice couple.

"Nancy told me about you. I certainly can say your request to take the baby bobcat came as quite a surprise to me. Are you sure you really want to do this?" Jack asked.

"Yes, I'm certain," I stated, emphatically.

"You'll be taking on a heck of a lot of responsibility. You do know that, don't you?

"Yes, I know," I said. "Where is the kitten?" I looked around the small living room area and then, as if on cue, the small animal walked out from behind

Parthur

the couch and sat down to look up at the three of us. He was all kitten, with big feet, fat body and plump legs. The markings on his face and the little tufts of fur on his ears definitely made him different from any domestic cat, however. I quickly bent down to the small animal. "Hi, Parthur." I held out my hand for the kitten to smell. He looked up and eyed me suspiciously, but then sniffed my fingers. He backed away then moved forward and sniffed them again. Then he reached over and licked them. I smiled as his rough tongue cleaned my little finger. I reached over and patted the top of his head. He didn't pull away from my contact.

"So, you already have a name for him," Jack said. "I've never heard of a name like that one before but I guess it's as good as any."

"All of us had a hand in the name." I nodded in the direction of the station wagon. "'I've got Kofa High School's four-girl golf team in the car. We've just come from a school golf trip to Phoenix. So 'par' became 'Parthur'." I stood up as the bobcat kitten wandered over to a little saucer that held some milk.

"I tried to find a clean box that was big enough to put him in for your trip back to Yuma," Jack said, as he removed his arm from around Nancy. "But I just couldn't find one big enough. Are you certain you still want to take him? I mean there are five of you in your car." If Jack had been honest with himself, he really was looking for some excuse to keep the small animal just a little longer.

I looked over at the small kitten. He had taken a few licks from the dish and was now cleaning his face with his front paw. He tilted his head and looked up at me with his sharp round eyes. His face was totally disarming. "Yes," I said, "I will take him. This is a dream come true." I quickly told Jack and Nancy about my encounter with Dr. Hibben's pet bobcat in college. "I really want to do right by this animal," I said earnestly. I was afraid maybe they had changed their minds.

Jack was impressed with my obvious commitment to the small animal. He had grown very fond of the kitten in the few days it had been in his and Nancy's care but he knew he and Nancy just could not and should not keep him.

"I promise I will do my best to take care of him,"

Jack and Nancy looked at each other and then back at me. "We know you will," Nancy said, "or we wouldn't be doing this."

I walked over to Parthur and bent over to pat his head again. The fur on top was so soft and silky. I then let the kitten smell my hand once more, and gently I stroked him down his back. He showed no fear of my touch and even licked my hand once more in appreciation of my soft pats. Finally, I reached down and carefully picked up the small animal with my hand under his tummy and cradled him in my arms. He never struggled. "Well, Parthur, are you ready to go home?" I looked down at the furry bundle then I started for the front door of the trailer. Jack quickly opened the door and the three of us plus one small animal stepped into the night and headed toward the station wagon.

The front lights of the vehicle made visibility quite clear for the four girls in the back seat of the station wagon and they watched with eager anticipation as I carried the small kitten toward the car. As I stopped at the driver's side door, I could see all four of their faces in the back seat, straining to get a glimpse of the little animal in my arms through the opened rear window. "Now everyone, sit very still," I instructed the girls. "I'm going to get in the front seat and I'll let him just walk around and get comfortable."

Jack nodded and added, "It is important no one gets excited, because then he will sense something is wrong and then he'll get excited."

For just a moment I stared at Jack. *My dad would have said something like that*, I thought. I turned and looked back at the four girls, "He's right. Everyone must stay calm." The four girls looked from me to Jack then to Parthur. Slowly they rolled up the back window, sat back in their seats and watched.

Jack opened the driver's side door for me. The overhead interior light of the vehicle came on, and all four girls leaned forward from the back seat to get a better look. I slipped in behind the steering wheel, still holding the bobcat kitten. Jack closed the door softly, and the overhead light went off. I placed Parthur on the front seat next to me, leaned forward and turned the inside light on again. All eyes were on the kitten to see what he would do.

The little bobcat stretched himself and looked around. Then he jumped up on the back of the front seat. I was amazed at how effortlessly and easily he made the jump. I turned and looked at the girls. "Remember, he is just a baby and is very curious. Don't make any sudden moves." All eyes in the back seat were watching the small bobcat perched on the top of the front seat.

Parthur looked around from his perch to the front seat and then the back seat and suddenly jumped into Amy's lap. She was sitting next to the window, and she jumped just a little in surprise, raising her hands in the air as he landed on her lap. He looked up at her and she reached out her hand and patted him tentatively. He liked it. He then moved across each of the girl's laps, and each girl in turn carefully touched his body.

"Oh, Miss Fritz, he is so soft." Beth cooed.

"And he is so cute," Amy offered. All the girls were murmuring to the small animal at once and were covering his head and back with soft pats as he moved from one to another.

Parthur liked all the attention but he quickly jumped to the back of the front seat again. His short little tail was switching back and forth. He looked to the front seat, then the back seat and then back to the front seat. He slid down into the front seat and sat down next to me. He looked up at me almost expectantly. I leaned over and gave his back a long swipe, from head to tail very softly. Then I patted him on his head several times.

Jack and Nancy had been watching from outside the car. Jack had his arm around Nancy's shoulders again. I rolled down the driver's side window halfway. "Well, I think we are ready to go."

Jack leaned down and looked in the window at the kitten, "You be good now, Parthur," he said rather wistfully. "Oh, I almost forgot," he continued. "He has a spot behind his right ear that he loves to have scratched."

"Thanks, I'll remember that." I detected a touch of sadness in his voice, for I could tell he would have loved to have kept the animal. I slowly rolled up the window, turned off the interior lights and started the engine. I looked back at the four girls again and smiled. I was extremely proud of them. "Well, girls, here we go." I looked down at the kitten by my side. He was completely at ease. I put the station wagon in reverse and slowly backed away from Nancy and Jack. Everyone waved goodbye. I put the large vehicle in gear and made a wide turn, and then we bumped back down the small gravel road leading away from the trailer park. I looked in the rear-view mirror, Jack and Nancy had not moved.

Parthur never left my side as I maneuvered the large station wagon through the dark back streets of Gila Bend. When we got on the highway heading to Yuma, the kitten yawned a couple of times, almost started to get into my lap, but then curled up next to me with his back touching the side of my leg.

He felt very secure with this young woman. He liked her voice and her pats. He had liked Nancy and Jack just fine but he sensed something special about Dawn. He closed his eyes listening to the soft purr of the engine and the low voices of Dawn and the girls, then he fell asleep.

The ride from Gila Bend to Yuma was exciting for everyone except the sleeping Parthur. The girls talked in hushed voices in the back seat so they wouldn't disturb the baby. Periodically, each of them leaned over the front seat to stroke his back. He looked so peaceful in the soft-white glow of the dashboard's lights. He didn't seem to mind their touches at all. He re-adjusted his sleeping position several times on the drive back to Yuma but, for the most part, he slept the whole way home.

It was almost midnight by the time I reached the outskirts of Yuma. I had discussed earlier where each of the girls lived. Kathy would be dropped off first. Beth and Carol were next door neighbors, so they left the car together. The kitten never moved from his curled-up sleeping position next to me as the doors opened and closed and the interior lights of the car went on and off as each of the girls left the car and retrieved their golf equipment. They all reached over to give him a final pat just before they exited the vehicle. Amy was the last one in the car. "Oh, Miss Fritz, he is so neat," she said in a hushed voice as she leaned on folded arms on the back of the front seat as I drove to her home. She reached over from the back seat and touched the back of the sleeping animal one more time as I drove up in front of her house.

    She jumped out of the car, closed the door swiftly and as quietly as she could and retrieved her golf clubs through the back window of the station wagon. She hoisted her clubs onto her shoulder and said, "Thanks again for being our 'coach.'" The front porch light was on at her home, and I watched her as she reached the front door. Amy turned and waved one more time, entered the dark house, closed the door and the front porch light went off. I turned the big station wagon around and headed for my apartment.

Parthur

Chapter 6

I lived in an apartment complex that bordered the middle of a long, par-five, golf fairway of Yuma Country Club. It was called the Fairway Apartments. I had a roommate, Berle Burt, but I hadn't given my roommate much thought up until now. I started to have some doubts as I drove through the sleepy, dark streets of Yuma to my apartment. How would Berle react to my new pet? Would she think having a bobcat as a pet was as great of an idea as I did? Could I convince her that there wasn't any danger? Was there any danger? Berle was a home economics teacher at Yuma High School. She and I had only just met that fall but we had become great friends almost immediately. She was a warm and friendly person with an infectious laugh. I knew Berle loved animals, but I just wasn't certain how she would respond to Parthur. Well, I would certainly find out soon enough.

Parthur was wide awake and sitting up by my side as I pulled under the carport at the back side of my apartment building. He sensed that something new was about to happen. I turned off the engine, pushed in the head light switch and took a deep breath. "Well, Parthur, we're at your new home." The little animal responded to my voice and licked my arm. I reached over the animal for my purse which was on the floor in front of the passenger seat. I put it in my lap and dug through it until I found the key to my apartment. I placed the key for the front door in my right hand, slung the shoulder strap of my purse over my left shoulder and then picked up the animal in my arms. I opened the car door, clumsily holding Parthur close to my chest, slid out of the station wagon's front seat and closed the car door by bumping my backside into it. Parthur never moved or squirmed in my arms but he watched everything around him as I made my way from the carport and walked through the breezeway to the inner courtyard of the apartments. Small lights built into the lower part of the walls lighted the way. My front door was the first apartment on the left, when I got to the courtyard.

Berle had left a light on in the living room of the apartment and its glow could be seen through the closed curtains of the big picture window next to the front door. No one was around in the large courtyard that featured a swimming pool in the center of the apartment building, and I was glad for that. I really didn't want to explain to any of my neighbors about my new pet, just now. I fumbled clumsily putting the key in the lock of the front door, because I didn't want to loosen my grip on Parthur. The key turned. I opened the door and slid quickly inside; closing the door quietly behind me.

When inside the apartment, I placed Parthur on the long, beige couch in the living room. He turned around, sat down on his haunches and looked at me expectantly. I backed away from the couch and stood there in the middle of the living room, staring at him for a minute and hesitated. Finally, I whispered to the sitting kitten, "I'd better go tell Berle about you," and I moved towards Berle's bedroom door.

I tapped lightly on the door. "Berle? Berle?" I called softly. My roommate was a sound sleeper. "Berle?" I called again just a little louder. Just then, Parthur let out a huge ally-cat yowl. It sounded as if a heavy object had fallen on his paw. I quickly looked back into the living room to see if he was all right. Parthur was still there on the beige couch but he was standing up now on all fours with his little short tail twitching back and forth.

He looked at me expectantly and cocked his head. It was the first time he had tried out his voice and he was pretty pleased with himself. For such a small animal, the sound certainly surprised me but the sound really surprised Berle.

"What was that?" She had jumped out of her bed and had rushed to open the bedroom door with rather a frightened look on her face.

"It's all right, it's all right," I hurriedly explained. Berle stood in the bedroom doorway, rubbing her eyes. She was trying to comprehend just what had awakened her out of a deep sleep. "Berle, I hope you are ready for this but I have a new pet," I went on excitedly.

"Wait a minute; I thought you were on a golf trip."

"I was," I went on. "But you aren't going to believe what I've brought home. He's in the living room. You've got to meet him, Berle. He is absolutely the most gorgeous and adorable animal ever."

After the sound Berle had heard coming from the living room, she hesitantly followed me and stood there speechless in the middle of the room when she saw Parthur. He was still standing on the couch, and he looked at Berle, then me, then Berle again.

"What is it?" Berle finally said, as I took her arm and led her closer to the couch and Parthur. Berle pulled away from me and hesitated a few feet from the couch. This animal was obviously from the cat family, but this wasn't like any cat Berle had ever seen. It didn't have a tail, or at least not much of a tail, and the markings on its face were so unusual but it obviously was a kitten and it was so cute.

"He's a baby bobcat. I think he is about five weeks old," I answered as I sat down next to Parthur on the couch. "He won't hurt you, Berle. Come and sit down next to him." Parthur sat back on his haunches and I leaned over and patted the seat on the other side of the kitten.

Berle sat down slowly next to Parthur, never taking her eyes off him. She reached out tentatively with one hand to touch him but, before her fingers touched his fur, Parthur leaned over and licked her hand. Any fear or apprehension Berle had felt left her immediately with that lick. She responded with a soft gentle pat to the kitten's head. As her hand swept down his back, Parthur arched to her touch and let out a funny little noise that sounded very much like a purr. "Oh, Dawn, he is adorable. Wherever did you find him?"

I quickly told Parthur's tale. I told how his mother had been shot, how Jack couldn't kill her baby and how I had met Nancy at the truck stop. I went on and recounted the story of Dr. Hibben's pet at the University of New Mexico. "Berle, it's a dream come true. I really want to do right by him."

As we talked, Parthur jumped off the couch and began surveying the room. He was wide awake now, and he wanted to explore. We stopped talking and followed him as he went from room to room in their apartment. He had a ravenous enthusiasm for his explorations and missed nothing. He went into every closet, under each bed and inspected the shower stall with some suspicion. He checked out the tall wastebasket in the kitchen by standing on his hind legs and looking in. When it fell over on top of him, he was caught underneath for just a few seconds. Berle and I jumped to his rescue. His little tail flicked back and forth when he was released from the big, white plastic cave. He was truly enjoying his reconnaissance of the apartment as we followed him. There were so many new smells and fun areas to explore.

Suddenly I exclaimed, "What are we going to do for his bathroom? I forgot to ask Nancy and Jack about that."

"Do you think he would use a sandbox?" Berle offered.

"Well, there is only one way to find out," I said. "You stay here and get acquainted with Parthur." I grabbed a large, shallow, cardboard box that had been sitting on the kitchen table, took out a big serving spoon from the silverware drawer and headed out the front door to the desert behind my car. It took some time to fill the box with the utensil I had selected but I used my hands as well and got the task done. I carried the heavy box filled with sand back into the apartment and placed it in the corner of our bathroom.

Parthur was in the kitchen with Berle, finishing a small saucer of milk. I picked him up, carried him to the bathroom and showed him the box. He sniffed it carefully, stepped in and immediately relieved himself and then promptly began to cover it up, just like any domestic cat. I sighed with relief. I couldn't believe how many traits of an ordinary house cat Parthur seemed to have but he definitely was different.

It was almost 2 o'clock in the morning by the time Berle and I finally got to bed that night. She closed the door to her room but I left mine open. Parthur was the last one to call it quits that first evening in our apartment and his new home. Just as I was about to drift off to sleep, he jumped up on the end of my bed. I sat up, reached down and patted him softly on his head. Then I remembered what Jack had told me about his itchy right ear. I leaned down and scratched it carefully, and he pushed his head into my hand with the pleasure of it. I then leaned back against the headboard of my bed and watched Parthur in the dim light, curious to see what he would do. He stood there for a few moments at the end of my bed and then turned around and around until he had his spot just right. He lay down on top of the covers and curled up with his body touching my right foot through the blankets. I was pleased that the young bobcat seemed to like and trust me. I reached down and patted him one more time. Parthur stretched in pleasure.

Parthur was content. This new place really felt like home. He liked Dawn and her touch. She seemed to genuinely like him, and he liked her. It was the first time since that awful day on the rock ledge he felt really safe and secure. The Copelands had been nice to him. They had fed him but they hadn't spent much time with him. They had kept him in a box at night but Dawn had allowed him his freedom. He liked it here at the end of her bed, and he dozed off into a sound and peaceful sleep.

I slid down from the headboard, leaned up and plumped my pillow and adjusted the covers. I listened to Parthur's breathing then I realized he wasn't breathing at all; he was purring. It felt good he had accepted me. I folded my hands behind my head and looked up at the dark ceiling. "I hope you'll be happy here," I whispered to the sleeping animal. And I then made a promise to him and myself that night. I would do my best to raise him as best I could, no matter what.

The young cat's breathing turned to a softer tone and I was certain that he was sound asleep. *I really think it's going to work*, I thought. I turned on my side, careful not to disturb sleeping Parthur, and finally drifted off to sleep myself.

Chapter 7

The next two weeks went by quickly. Parthur settled into his new surroundings and home and he really seemed to enjoy the two of us but because I lavished so much attention on him, I was by far his favorite. The memory of his real mother was being rapidly replaced by me.

Parthur learned to anticipate our schedules quickly during the school week. When either Berle or I returned home from our teaching day, Parthur always seemed to be waiting just inside the front door, ready to play and roughhouse. He loved to play hide and seek with us. We would chase him or he would chase us all over the apartment. He would feign attacks from behind the couch or from under one of our beds. More than once, though, he caught

Berle or me off guard with a sudden mock attack. A blur of tawny-yellow spotted fur would come streaking out of his hiding place and he would grab us around our ankles with his paws, his claws partially retracted. Parthur delighted in his play and, when he wasn't chasing after the two of us, he leaped and chased phantom playmates all over the apartment.

He was so agile and quick and always his short little tail flashed back and forth; it was dazzling white on its underside and black barred on its surface. Even though Parthur tried to be careful with his claws and baby teeth, it seemed as if Berle and I always had little red welts and scratches on our legs and arms from our play times together. He definitely had razor sharp claws.

There were lots of quiet times as well. Whenever I graded papers on the couch in the living room, this seemed to be Parthur's signal that maybe he could get some good scratching from me. He would jump up on the couch next to me and press his body under the papers I was reading and grading until he was in my lap. He would nudge my hand until I would finally put down what I was doing to give him my undivided attention. He loved to be stroked from his head down his back, and, oh, how he loved to have his ears scratched, especially that right one. If I stopped too soon, he would lick my hands anxiously to ask for more.

The Fairway Apartments, where Berle and I lived, did allow pets; however, the two of us decided it was prudent to keep Parthur's existence our secret. After a week and a half with Parthur in our apartment, no one else who lived in the apartments knew he was there. Our unit was on the first floor of the two-story apartment complex by the end of the large pool that filled the center of the "U" shaped building. Each day while Berle and I were at our respective schools, we made certain our drapes on the large front picture window were pulled together securely.

The apartment manager, Mrs. Winslow, was a persnickety, plump woman in her late forties. She was a suspicious woman. Many times, Berle and I had caught her peeking out from behind the curtains in her apartment kitchen window, which was located kitty-corner across the center courtyard from our apartment. Mrs. Winslow always seemed to be interested in what we were doing, when we returned home from school each day, and especially when a date would arrive for either one of us. The two of us felt Mrs. Winslow didn't trust us and was convinced we were going to throw a wild party any day now. No matter what we said or did, we couldn't shake Mrs. Winslow's suspicious opinions of us. It was probably because we were young, not married and just out of college.

This manager was much more solicitous around her winter renters, who made up a large proportion of the Fairway apartment dwellers, who were all of retirement age and paid double for the same apartments as ours. Berle and I had signed a rental contract for a year, so that was why our rent was so much lower. The winter renters leased their apartments for only six to seven months during the winter season. Yuma was a winter haven in the sixties for visitors from up north. They flocked to the daily sunshine that Yuma offered, and spent the winter months soaking up the warm rays. The Fairway Apartments were always filled to capacity from early October to late April with these "snowbirds". Mrs. Winslow would fawn over her winter renters and would barely speak to Berle or me when they were around. The two of us were by far the youngest renters in the apartment complex.

I had another reason for not wanting Mrs. Winslow to know I had Parthur in our apartment. Mrs. Winslow was deathly afraid of cats, even kittens. About a month earlier, our next-door neighbor had gotten a small kitten for a pet. I had been invited in to see the new addition and, as the door opened, the little calico kitten made a dash for freedom out to the pool area. Mrs. Winslow was standing in the doorway of the laundry room and the kitten made a beeline for her, blocking her exit from that room. Everyone was stunned by the shrieks coming from the woman. She stamped her feet, flapped her arms and screamed. The kitten stood there looking up at this rather large, flapping human, in confusion. Finally, the kitten's owner scooped it up and took it back into her apartment. Later, behind closed doors, everyone did have a huge laugh over the incident. It seemed awfully silly someone so large could be so frightened of something so small and cute. Obviously, I didn't even want to imagine what would happen if Mrs. Winslow knew about Parthur.

When Berle and I went off to school each morning, the young bobcat would usually spend the day napping. On one morning, however, Parthur's existence in our apartment was no longer to be a secret. On that particular day as I was about to leave, Parthur was curled up on the sofa and was ready to take a nap. I looked over at him from the front door and walked back to the couch to give him a quick pat on his head. "Be good. See you later." I then turned, headed to the door but quickly walked over to the curtains at the big picture window and made an adjustment to make sure they were completely closed. I looked over at Parthur one last time then left. As I stepped out our front door, no one was around the pool area. It was too early. I was off to school.

Chapter 8

Parthur watched as Dawn left the apartment with half closed eyes. When she was gone, he gave his body a big, long stretch, yawed a wide-mouthed yawn that showed all his sharp baby teeth and curled back up to take a long nap. It was probably about two hours later when the noise outside that big, curtain-covered, picture window would not let him sleep one minute more. He looked up and scrutinized the long, beige, heavy material that covered the glass. What he was hearing was just on the other side. He was just going to have to investigate.

The center courtyard of the Fairway Apartments had a swimming pool with a diving board positioned right in front of Dawn and Berle's front door. On this morning, a large crowd of winter visitors were grouped around the pool area and several of the men were trying out their diving techniques, in particular, the cannon ball. The noise was just too irresistible to Parthur as he heard large splashes of water over and over again and many humans talking and laughing. He had to see what was going on outside the apartment.

He immediately jumped off the sofa to investigate. He stood in front of the curtained window and listened. He heard more splashes. He definitely had to see what was out there. He batted at the fabric of the long curtains and he watched as they swayed back and forth but he still could see nothing. Then Parthur decided to "nose" the curtains aside so he could look out the window. He tried to fit his head under the heavy drapes and lift up but he didn't like the weight of the fabric on his face. He backed off. More splashes. He would just have to try it again. Finally, he managed to get his face between the curtains and the wall. The glass window was just above him. He shook the drapes away from his body, stood on his hind legs and pulled up his upper torso with his paws placed firmly on the windowsill. He looked out on a great view of the center courtyard and its shimmering pool. His sharp, round eyes watched with interest first one diver and then another. He loved the big splashes they made when they hit the water.

It wasn't long before someone noticed him. "Look." shouted Jim, one of the divers. "There's a wild animal in that apartment." Jim was standing on the end of the diving board with his finger pointing at

Dawn and Berle's window. Everyone in the patio area turned and stared in that direction.

"What is it?" one woman asked, as she stood up from her seat to get a better view. She was certain it wasn't a domestic cat. The ears were wrong. They were black at the tips with little white tufts on the ends. Also, the striping on the face was most unusual. It radiated from his nose into muttonchops on each side of his cheeks. She had never seen any domestic cat with those markings. "Is it some kind of wild cat?" she asked.

"I'm not sure," said Jim, as he bent down and steadied himself on the end of the diving board to get a better look.

"I think I know what it is." An elderly white-haired man rose from his chair and took a few steps toward the window to get a closer and better view. He studied the young cat's face from across the pool. "Why, it's a young bobcat." Everyone in the pool area stared in the direction of Parthur. There was a stunned silence. "But what would he be doing in there?" the white-haired man continued. "Doesn't that apartment belong to those two young teachers?"

"Do you think they know it is there?" asked the woman again. "Maybe it got in there after they left for work this morning."

"How could it have gotten in there after they left? There is no back door," said the white-haired man.

"Well, I'm going to go get Mrs. Winslow," said Jim, as he stepped off the diving board. He grabbed a towel to pat himself dry as he headed in the direction of the manager's apartment.

Parthur loved all the attention. He looked from one shocked face to another as they all moved from around the pool and drew closer to his window. He liked it better, though, when they were all moving around, jumping in the pool and splashing water. Now, they were just staring at him and there wasn't a lot for him to see. He dropped down from the window, leaving everyone looking at the back of swaying drapes.

Within five minutes Jim and Mrs. Winslow were walking back toward Dawn and Berle's apartment. She was carrying a long-handled broom, and as she got closer to the apartment her steps got slower and slower and she lagged behind Jim. "Just exactly what did you see?" she asked him.

"Well, I'm not certain but it did look like some kind of wild animal. Bill thought it was a bobcat."

"Bill, is that right? You thought it was a bobcat?" Bill was standing in the center of a group gathered in front of the apartment window.

"Yep, sure did look like one to me but it was a young one."

Mrs. Winslow crept closer to Dawn and Berle's window with her broom poised in front of her. She dreaded what she might see but the window was completely empty, and she was relieved. Everyone started to talk at once.

"Well, I saw it," one woman stated flatly. "Didn't you see it, Mildred?"

"I sure did."

"We know something is in there because we all saw it," said Mildred's husband. Suddenly there was movement among the curtains again. All conversation ceased as everyone watched in disbelief.

Parthur, hearing all the talking just outside the window, decided it was time to investigate again. This time he was able to maneuver the curtains a lot quicker. It took him only a couple of seconds before he was back in the picture window with his front paws on the windowsill again. Everyone stared at him with shocked looks. When the young cat appeared, they all took a few steps backwards.

"I was right," said Bill. "It is a young bobcat."

"He doesn't look at all scared of us," said Mildred.

"What do you think, Mrs. Winslow? Do you think those two teachers know he is in there? He certainly doesn't act frightened of us," Bill said as he moved closer to the window and leaned down examining the young cat. He tapped on the glass just above the animal's head. Parthur took a playful swipe at the hand that was on the other side of the window.

Mrs. Winslow was horrified. It was a cat. Not an ordinary cat, either. It was some kind of wild cat. She tried to get control by convincing herself she was safe. After all, he was behind the glass of the window but it was a wild animal. She took a few deep breaths and swallowed several times before she was certain her voice wouldn't crack with fear before she spoke, "I'm sure those girls know about that animal," she said, as she backed away from the window. "I'll certainly have to have a talk with them when they return from work today." There was no way she was going to use her master key to check on the inside of Dawn and Berle's apartment and she backed away even faster, using her broom as a shield. As soon as she reached her apartment, she hesitated for just a minute, turned to look back in the direction of the girls' apartment then whirled around and made a hasty retreat behind the safety of her door, leaving the small excited group watching the young cat.

Parthur grew weary of looking at the shocked faces outside his window and, once again, dropped down from in front of the curtains. The swimming pool group stood in front of Dawn and Berle's window for some time, waiting for him to return but, when he didn't, they slowly ambled back to their chairs around the diving board and the pool.

The presence of the small bobcat in the teachers' apartment was the topic of conversation all day around the pool and, as new people joined the band of sun-worshipers, they were immediately filled in with the details of his appearances. All afternoon, the residents of the apartments kept their eyes on that one picture window as they lounged in the deck chairs they'd placed facing the apartment.

Several more times Parthur appeared. "Look, there he is again," someone would yell. Parthur seemed to love the excitement that each one of his appearances caused.

The crowd around that area of the pool and his window had become quite large by late afternoon. Periodically, Mrs. Winslow peeked out from behind the curtains of her kitchen window to watch the activities at the pool. She shivered each time she thought about that strange cat in an apartment so close to hers but she wasn't going to step outside that door.

Chapter 9

It was about 4 o'clock when I returned home from school. As I left my car, I could hear excited conversations from the pool area. I wondered what could be going on. There was always activity around that area but this seemed different. As I turned the corner from the walkway to my apartment, my heart sank. There I saw a large group of excited residents gathered in front of my window. I didn't have to guess the reason why.

Mrs. Winslow had been waiting for me. She had been watching from her favorite spying position at her kitchen window. As soon as I appeared, Mrs. Winslow was at her door. "Dawn," she yelled from across the courtyard. "What do you have in that apartment?" Her hands were on her hips and she was trying to sound stern and brave but there was a quiver of fear in her voice. She stood in her doorway with her hand gripping the knob tightly for a quick retreat. There was no way she was going to leave the safety of her apartment for this conversation.

The group in front of my front window all turned and looked in the direction of Mrs. Winslow then they all turned and stared at me, waiting for my answer. "Why, just a baby kitten." I was trying to sound nonchalant.

"What kind of kitten?"

"Well," I stalled a bit. I looked from Mrs. Winslow to the group at my window then back to Mrs. Winslow. "Well, I guess I would have to say that he is a baby bobcat." I sort of mumbled the word "bobcat."

"What kind of baby?" Mrs. Winslow demanded again.

I sighed and spoke a little louder, "A baby bobcat." A hush had fallen on the group of residents who were looking on. "Look, his mother was shot and killed, so I took him in. He really is quite harmless." I moved toward the little group in front of my apartment. They obviously were not afraid because they were all trying to get a glimpse of him.

Mrs. Winslow had now ventured a few feet out of the door of her residence. She took a few more steps toward me, thought about it and then stopped. "You know you will be held responsible for any damage that animal does to that apartment."

"Yes, I know, Mrs. Winslow."

Mrs. Winslow opened her mouth to say something else then decided against it. She looked long and hard at me then she quickly went back to her apartment and slammed the door.

I turned back to the other apartment residents gathered at my front door and picture window. As I joined the group everyone had questions.

"Is he dangerous?"

"Aren't you afraid he will hurt you?" Mildred quizzed me.

"How old is he?" Bill asked. He was feeling pretty proud of himself because he was the one who had known what the animal was all along.

The questions came tumbling out one after another. Finally, I held up my hands. "Whoa, wait a minute." Everyone stopped and waited for me to continue. "He is perfectly harmless. In fact, I think he has adopted me as his mother." It amazed me how frightened people could be of a young bobcat. Fear was not a reaction that had ever occurred to me. I gave the group a quick synopsis of how I came to adopt him. They all nodded and murmured their support. I hesitated for a minute. "Would you like to come in and meet him?"

Not all of them thought this was a great idea and that group quickly moved away and went back to their respective apartments but four, Bill, Jim, Mildred and her husband, Alex, were eager to meet my exotic pet.

"Let me go in first to make sure he doesn't get too excited," I said. "He hasn't had any visitors before." I went inside. Parthur greeted me just inside the door. I leaned down to give his head a quick pat. "Well, you certainly caused a big stir today." Parthur seemed pleased with himself and shook his short tail back and forth. "Are you ready for some visitors?"

As if on cue, he jumped to the sofa and sat down on his haunches expectantly. I crossed to the picture window and pulled the drapes open. All four of our guests peered in. I opened the door, "All right, he's ready for visitors. Why don't you come in by pairs? Who wants to be first?"

"Bill, you and Jim go in first. My husband and I will wait," Mildred said. "We'll watch from the window."

Bill and Jim tentatively followed me into the apartment. Parthur was still sitting on the couch as if he had been expecting visitors. I sat down next to Parthur and put a reassuring hand on his back; Bill sat on the other side. Jim remained standing.

"Can I pet him?" Bill asked.

"Certainly," I answered. "He loves to be patted on his head and then stroked down his back." I showed him how to do it. "If you would like to scratch his ears, he loves to be itched, especially behind his right one." Bill started to stroke the young anima, and Parthur closed his eyes with pleasure. Jim leaned in and did some scratching behind that itchy right ear. Parthur loved that, as well.

"How did you know he was here in the apartment?" I asked.

The two men explained how Parthur had evidently wiggled up in between the curtains and the window to watch what was going on at the patio and around the swimming pool.

"I don't think Mrs. Winslow is very happy about your pet," Jim added.

"That's for sure. You know, she is afraid of cats?"

"I had heard."

Parthur

"I really admire what you are doing for him but you've certainly got your hands full," Bill said as he rose from the couch to leave. Jim joined him.

"I know." I followed Bill and Jim to the door.

The two men left, and Mildred and her husband came in to meet the baby bobcat. Parthur was still sitting on the couch and he watched with interest as the two of them approached. Mildred tentatively sat on the couch next to Parthur with her hands folded neatly in her lap. I sat on the other side. Alex, her husband, stood in front of the cat. "Would you like to pet him, Mildred?"

Mildred was a petite, white-haired lady in her late seventies. She sat stiffly next to Parthur but she had a soft look on her face as she looked down at the baby bobcat next to her. "No, it really is quite a thrill to just sit next to him," she said. "He really is most remarkable." Parthur looked up at her then he reached over and licked her arm just once. Mildred didn't jump at his touch but she smiled a huge smile at his acceptance of her. She never attempted to touch him and her hands remained in her lap for the whole visit.

As Mildred and her husband were leaving, Berle arrived home from her school. "What happened?" she asked.

I told her of Parthur's discovery. "You should have seen the look on Mrs. Winslow's face. I don't think she will ever come anywhere near this apartment ever again." Both of us laughed. "Well, I guess we don't have to keep the drapes pulled any more. Looks like the whole world knows he's here now."

The next day was Saturday, and the drapes were wide open in the large picture window on the front of our apartment. I positioned a small table in the middle of the window for Parthur to sit on, and he immediately took his position there. He watched with great interest all the comings and goings in the courtyard.

Bill walked by. As soon as he saw Parthur on his new perch, he leaned down, so he was at eye level with the animal. He tapped on the window softly, and Parthur responded by patting the inside of the window with his paw at Bill's hand. Bill smiled and looked up as he saw me approaching behind the cat. He waved, and I waved back. He gave a "thumbs up" as he walked away. Then I had a great idea. I rummaged around the apartment until I found a small piece of poster board. Carefully I lettered on it, **BEWARE OF THE CAT**. I giggled as I placed it on the windowsill next to Parthur's table.

Parthur immediately became the favorite of almost everyone who lived in the Fairway Apartments. Well, almost everyone. Certainly not Mrs. Winslow. Most of the residents never visited him in person but they did spend lots of time with him at his window. The young cat spent hours at his window perch and enjoyed all the visits. I was glad he had something to fill his idle time while I was teaching. Mrs. Winslow, however, never dropped by.

Chapter 10

It was by accident I discovered Parthur loved to ride in cars. Parthur and I had been having one of our great hide-and-seek games one Saturday morning. When I had thought the game was over and leaving to go on errands, I was ambushed by my pet as I walked by the partially opened coat closet door on my way out of the apartment. Parthur was not ready to give up the game. He grabbed me around my ankles softly with his paws and just didn't want to let loose.

"Parthur, I have to go and get gas in my car." I dropped down on my knees beside him and rubbed his head and back. He licked my hands in appreciation of my attention. Berle had left for an appointment hours before, so it was just the two of us there in the apartment. I hated to leave my pet all alone on a Saturday, since I had to leave him all by himself during the school week but the gas tank was dangerously low. I knew I could make it to the gas station but maybe not to the high school on Monday morning. Now all Parthur wanted to do was play. "Wait a minute; I'll just take you along."

    I grabbed my purse then picked up Parthur and headed for the front door of the apartment. I opened the door a crack and looked both ways. No one was in the center courtyard or around the pool. I looked across the courtyard to see if Mrs. Winslow was peeking out her window. It looked all clear. I took a deep breath, rushed through the door, walked quickly with Parthur held firmly in my arms and headed straight for my car. We met no one.

    Quickly, I opened the driver's side door and tossed Parthur across into the passenger seat of my little 1960, German, Karmann Ghia. I laughed out loud with relief that no one had spotted us and jumped into the driver's seat and closed the door. Parthur sat in the front seat and looked up at me expectantly. I reached over and patted him on his head, then started the engine and backed out of the carport.

    Parthur loved that car ride. It wasn't the same as the night I had brought him home. The sun was out and there was so much to see. He immediately started jumping from the front seat to the small back seat as I made my way out of the parking lot and headed toward the gas station. He checked out the views from each window and tried to stand in the back window well, but the constant starts and stops of the automobile in traffic made it difficult for him to hold his position but, by the time I reached the gas station, Parthur had positioned himself on the back of the driver's seat with his body pressed into the back of my head and neck for stability. He had discovered very quickly this was the best position for viewing the sights that were flying by. He tried not to miss a thing. His head whipped back and forth as he tried to keep track of everything, as it moved past him.

As my little beige car drove up next to the gas pump, Parthur was facing toward the driver's side window. The owner, Al, was just finishing with the car on the other side of the pump. He knew me and recognized my car. He nodded in my direction but it was obvious he had not noticed my passenger yet. When he was finished, he ambled over to my car. "Well, little lady, what can I do for you this fine morning?" Al asked, then he saw Parthur. He stood there dumbfounded with his mouth open then he slowly took a couple of steps backward. "Whoa. Wait a minute." He pointed at Parthur and said, "That's a wild animal you've got there."

I started to roll down my window. "Stop. Roll up that window," Al yelled with his hands outstretched in front of him.

"He won't hurt you. He's just my new pet, Al." I did oblige Al, however, by rolling up my window except for two inches. "Isn't he gorgeous?" I smiled at him.

Al was stunned. He was almost sixty and he had owned this gas station for twenty years. He had seen a lot of strange things in people's cars but this was by far the strangest sight he had ever seen. Parthur looked at him from his perch behind my head through the window and sensed his fear. His little tail whipped back and forth as the two of them stared at each other.

"Dawn, you just keep that window of yours up," Al finally said. "I have a healthy respect for those animals. Are you certain you are safe?" he asked, incredulously.

"He's just like an overgrown kitten, Al. Honestly, he won't hurt you."

"Well, if you are sure you're all right," Al replied. He circled my car so he stayed as far away as he could from the window where Parthur was situated. Carefully, he took the nozzle from the gas pump and placed it into my tank while he leaned away from the car. Parthur jumped to the back seat for a better view of what he was doing. Twice Parthur batted at the window nearest Al. Both times, Al jumped.

"Parthur." I scolded. "Don't do that." I could see the fear in the man and Parthur was taking advantage of the situation. Parthur sensed the man was deathly afraid of him. He was acting like a bad child and tormenting the man. I leaned into the back seat and coaxed the animal back to the front. Al was relieved.

When the tank was filled with gas, I pushed the money through the small opening in the window to Al. He stepped away from my car quickly. As I drove away, I could see him staring after us in my rearview mirror.

I never took Parthur back to the gas station again because of my respect for Al. The aggression that Parthur showed when he sensed the fear in Al did bother me. It was like some primal knowledge deep in Parthur's brain that let him see his advantage when he sensed fear in someone.

Parthur and I did take many drives around the little town of Yuma. Always, Parthur's position was behind my head on the back of the driver's seat looking out the windows. In those early months, his size was not what caught people's attention. Except for the powerful hind quarters, he was the size of a large domestic cat. It was the distinctive striping on his face and body, the short tail and the fur tufts that decorated his black and white ears that made people take a second look. The white spot on the back of each of his ears gave the young animal the appearance of having rearview eyes, and he could swivel them forward, almost making himself look as if he had four eyes.

Long "stop and go" lights always seemed to cause the most problems. Drivers and passengers of cars stopped next to me at the same red light would glance over at Parthur and me. At first, all they would see was a large cat perched on the back of the driver's seat behind a young woman's head. Then they would take a second glance. That's when the excited looks and pointing would begin. Many times, my car was the only one to move when the light turned green.

Parthur learned a trick quite by accident one day. I had a stiff hairbrush I used to brush his coat. Parthur loved it when I would groom him. On one occasion, when I stopped brushing his fur, Parthur patted his front right foot three times and looked at me expectantly for me to brush him some more. I gave him the 'thumbs up' sign and started brushing him again. Then I stopped. He did it again, he tapped his front paw three times and looked at me. I gave the 'thumbs up' sign again and brushed. I stopped. He tapped. This time, I didn't brush but just made the 'thumbs up' sign. He tapped. I laughed out loud and hugged the animal and, of course, obliged him with more brushing. We practiced his new trick several more times. He never missed once.

Berle had been out shopping that day, and when she walked in the door, I said, "Watch this." I made the 'thumbs up' sign, and immediately Parthur tapped the ground three times with his front, right paw.

"How did you ever get him to do that?" Berle was amazed.

"It really was just by accident." Just to make sure, I retrieved my hairbrush and gave him some more good strokes.

I stopped and gave him the 'thumbs up' sign again. Parthur repeated it again: pat, pat, pat. Berle and I both laughed

"Let me try it," Berle said. She raised her hand in the 'thumbs up' position. Parthur looked at her then he looked back at me but his paws never moved. Then I made the 'thumbs up' sign. Parthur obliged, tap, tap, tap.

"That is truly amazing," Berle said. "You two have your own special code." I leaned over and hugged Parthur again in appreciation of our special bond.

Parthur liked it when he pleased me and he never forgot the trick.

I was always looking for playthings for Parthur. I brought home balls, rubber toys that would squeak and all sorts of stuffed animals for Parthur to play with. He loved all these things but many of them were no match for his sharp teeth and claws. Sooner or later, they ended up in little pieces. One day, however, I brought home a soft, brown teddy bear with large eyes and soft silky short fur. It was love at first sight for Parthur. He was so gentle with it. He would clean it for hours with his rough little tongue, and he would carry it from room to room with great care. I found him many times curled up with his teddy bear for a nap. Never did he tear it up as his other toys. This was special. I thought maybe it was like a surrogate brother or sister to him or maybe it reminded him of his lost mother. At any rate, it brought comfort to him and that made me happy.

Chapter 11

The months flew by and, suddenly, it was early April. Parthur had grown considerably bigger over those months. He was now the size of a small dog. I had tried to keep Parthur on cat food but it had become clear early on he was a meat eater. Berle and I used a local butcher shop for our cooking needs, and I had told the owner, Harry, about my pet. He always saved special, large bones for Parthur to gnaw on and sold them to me at a special rate but, the young bobcat's favorite food, however, was raw chicken.

Harry knew I took Parthur for rides. "How about coming by my shop one day. I'd love to see and meet your pet." He was intrigued by my unorthodox ward. Soon after that invitation, I drove the young animal by the butcher shop one Saturday morning and was lucky enough to find a parking place right in front of his store. I ran in the shop to tell Harry Parthur was out in the car and I was parked right out front. Harry was wrapping up a meat order for one of two customers waiting in front of the big glass meat case that filled one end of the small shop. Harry was a big, jolly man with an infectious, happy demeanor. He laughed with pleasure as he told his two customers, "You should see what this little lady has as a pet. Why, she has a baby bobcat." The two customers looked curiously at me. "As soon as I am done with you folks, she's going to introduce me to him." He laughed good-naturedly again.

"I'll wait for you outside, Harry." I left the butcher shop and stood by my car. Harry's customers exited the butcher shop one by one and both of them eyed me and the bobcat inside my car with curiosity. They hesitated for a moment then hurriedly went on their way. As Harry strolled out of the front door of his shop, he was wiping his hands on the end of a white towel. He threw the towel over his shoulder and walked around and around my car looking at the bouncing and active animal within as I stood by the driver's door. "He's really something, Dawn. What a beautiful animal."

"Would you like to pet him, Harry?"

"Gosh, I'd love to. Is it safe?" For one of the first times that I could remember, Harry had gotten rather serious.

"Sure," I answered. Harry had shown no fear of the animal, just respect. "Would you like to get in the car with him, or would you prefer to pet him through the window?"

"I think I'll take the window option," Harry laughed, just a little nervously. "I've washed my hands, but with all this meat smell on me, I wouldn't want him to mistake me for one of my steaks."

I got into the passenger side of the car with Parthur in the front driver's seat. I leaned over him and opened the driver's side window halfway. Parthur hopped to the back seat and then back to the front, driver's seat. He sat dawn and stretched his nose inquisitively toward the big man who was standing outside the half-opened window. Harry tentatively reached through the opening and extended his hand so Parthur could get his scent. Parthur closed his eyes and smelled the big hand. His sensitive nose picked up the smells of the butcher shop, and without any hesitation, the cat started licking Harry's hand. Harry was amazed at the feel of the animal's tongue on his fingers and he smiled and laughed nervously. Then he reached further in the open window and patted the young cat on his head. Parthur stood perfectly still. Harry laughed again and gave Parthur another pat on the head and then stroked him down his back. "He really is something, Dawn." he said again.

The bobcat liked Harry instantly. He sensed the big man was not afraid of him and he loved the smells he had found on his hand as he tried to lick Harry's fingers clean.

"He probably smells all that good meat I work with." He laughed again.

Hopkins

After that visit, Harry made sure Dawn always had the best deal possible on all her chicken orders.

Parthur

Chapter 12

The previous fall, Berle had registered with a local dog breeder of champion Chihuahuas, Don Stockley, to get a six-week-old pup. Berle really didn't want a show dog but Don was well known for breeding intelligent and good-natured puppies. Berle had asked him to let her know when he might have a pup that wasn't up to show quality but one that had good promise to be a great pet. The phone call from that breeder came on a Saturday morning in mid-April. Berle turned to me at the end of the conversation. "That was Don Stockley."

I looked at her with a questioning look.

"He's the one I ordered a Chihuahua pup from last fall."

I nodded when I remembered the name. I was sitting on the couch grading papers with Parthur at my side. He had turned over on his back and was begging me to scratch his tummy. "Great. I know you have been looking forward to getting one; especially one from one of his champion females. What did he say?"

"Dawn, he said I could have one in two weeks," Berle said.

"Two weeks. Yikes. I thought you were going to get one in late June after school was out, and Parthur and I would be gone." I paused for a moment. "There's no way that a small Chihuahua puppy and Parthur could ever live together here in this small apartment."

"I know," Berle answered miserably. "This particular puppy has just become available and I'm the first one he's called. If I don't take this one, I'll probably have to wait another year because he has a long list of people after my name. This is the first puppy he's had like this in almost a year and a half."

"But what can we do?" I asked. "Parthur is definitely a meat eater. I'm afraid your little dog would look like a large mouse to him. Food on the hoof."

"I know you are planning on taking Parthur home with you to Illinois in the spring to your parent's home."

"Yes, but that's in June, and it's only April now."

"Do you think there is any way you could send him to your parents a month early?" Berle ventured.

Parthur

"I don't know." I thought about that. "I guess I could. I'll have to give them a call later."

Parthur had now turned over and was sitting up next to me on the couch. He watched us with interest and he sensed that it had something to do with him.

At the end of the school year, I had planned on returning with Parthur to my parents' home located in Illinois near the Quad Cities: Moline, East Moline, Rock Island and Davenport, Iowa. My parents, Bee and Ken Fritz, lived on forty acres of virgin timber land along the Mississippi River between Hampton and Port Byron, Illinois. They had converted a summer home located on the property to an all-season residence back in the early 40's. This log cabin-style home was situated on the top of a prominent hill that overlooked the river running in front of the forty acres. The hill was so unusual local archaeologists in the area felt it might have been used as a burial hill for one of the Sauk Indian chiefs or maybe even the famous warrior, Black Hawk, back when this area had been Indian country. Bee and Ken Fritz liked the idea they might have a famous Indian buried in their front yard, so they never allowed any archaeological digs to disprove the theory. The Fritzes had lovingly named the forty-acre acreage, Hawthorn Hill, because of the preponderance of English Hawthorn Trees on the property. Surrounding the back of the Fritz's land was the Illiniwek Forest Preserve, covering hundreds of acres.

I had talked to my parents many times about my new pet and they knew I planned to return home to Illinois that summer with him. My father, Ken, was a man of the outdoors and loved all manner of wildlife. My mother, Bee, shared that same love with him. Both of them understood why I had adopted this baby bobcat.

When I was a little girl growing up on Hawthorn Hill, I had watched and helped my father many times with hurt and lost wild baby animals. It seemed as if there were always boxes or cages with small animals in them around the Fritz household the family was nursing back to health. Neighbors from many miles around brought their hurt wild things to the Fritz home. My parents' reputation for healing and returning wild things back to nature was well known throughout the community.

I lovingly remembered my father's huge hands that could be so soft and gentle to a little bird that had fallen out of its nest or that could fix a broken wing or feed a small bunny until it could be on its own. One spring Ken found a small crow that the blue jays were trying to kill. The baby crow had fallen out of a high nest, and its parents had abandoned the little bird. It was almost starved to death but Ken brought it home, fed it and nursed it back to health. The family had a pet crow that summer we named "Karl." That black bird was such fun. He rode on all of our shoulders, stole all sorts of shiny things from each of us but when fall arrived he flew off to be with his own kind.

One spring, when I was ten, my father had me fill a black and white composition notebook with a leaf from every tree and plant that we could find in the woods, even poison ivy. He had me label each page with the common name then we looked up the botanical name of each item. It is still one of my most

Parthur

beloved possessions. My dad loves animals and he had passed his love and compassion of all things wild to me. So, it was of no surprise to my parents I had taken on an orphaned bobcat. They were looking forward to my return home in June with Parthur.

That night I made the phone call to my parents about sending Parthur home ahead of me. My dad answered. I explained the upcoming arrival of Berle's new puppy. My father agreed Parthur and the new puppy would probably not be able to live together. "Dad," I said, "if I sent you Parthur by air, would you take care of him until I could get there in June?"

"Sure, Dawn, but I'm not sure how Parthur will handle that flight. You had better check with a local vet to see if there is anything you could give him to sedate him so that he can handle the trip with as little stress as possible."

"You're right." I had been certain my dad would be receptive to the idea of keeping Parthur for me until I could get back to my parents' home. My dad was right, however, I would have to search out a vet to see what he might recommend.

"And, Dawn," my dad continued, "have you given any thought to Parthur's future? What are you going to do when he becomes an adult bobcat? That's not far off, you know."

I knew I should be thinking ahead for Parthur but, somehow, I just couldn't imagine him as a full-grown bobcat. I knew my dad was concerned for my safety as well as that of my pet but I just couldn't visualize that Parthur could ever be a threat to me. "I know, Dad. When I get home this summer, we will have to discuss all that." Right now, all I wanted was to solve Parthur's immediate problem. The future would just have to wait. "I'll call a vet right away. I'll call you back when I know what flight he will be on."

"All right, Dawn."

"Dad, thanks a lot." I hung up the phone with a sigh and turned to my roommate who was sitting at the kitchen table. "Well, Berle, my dad says he will take him."

"Someday I would love to meet your parents, Dawn. I don't think I could call my mom or dad and tell them I was sending home a wild bobcat for them to take care of."

I smiled. "Yeah, they are pretty special people. I paused for a minute as I thought about my mom and dad back in Illinois and then continued, "My dad thinks I should see a vet about some sort of sedative to give Parthur to make the trip easier for him. Didn't I hear you talking the other day about a vet who had an office down in the valley?"

"That was Dr. Ben Wright," Berle answered. "I'll get you his phone number."

"Thanks, Berle, I'll call him Monday."

Parthur

Chapter 13

I called Dr. Wright the following Monday on my lunch hour. I related to him a quick history of how I had acquired Parthur and then I told him what I thought I needed. He was just a little surprised at my request. "I could come by your office this afternoon after I finish my classes, if it would be all right with you," I said.

"Could you bring your bobcat with you?" Dr. Wright asked. "I'd like to see his size and assess his health."

"Sure, no problem. He loves to ride in the car."

"Please don't bring him into the office, though," Dr. Wright quickly added. "I'm not sure how the rest of my patients would feel about a wild animal in the waiting room."

"No problem. I'll leave him in the car. You can take a look at him there."

I rushed back to my apartment that Monday afternoon as soon as I could break away from the students who were lingering after my last English literature class. When I reached the Fairway Apartments and passed the big picture window of my apartment, Parthur was sitting on his table watching for me. As I opened the door, he met me with several rubs against my legs.

"We are off for a little excursion," I looked down and told the animal. I threw my books and papers onto the kitchen table and scooped up the bobcat into my arms. "We're going for a ride." It always amazed me how Parthur never struggled when I carried him from one place to another. He had never tried to get out of my arms or squirmed to get free when I held him. I had seen many pictures of mother bobcats carrying their young in their mouths, and their babies didn't seem to struggle either. I was certain Parthur had accepted me as his mother, maybe that was why he always trusted me and stayed so calm in my arms.

I walked out the door with Parthur, which now had become a familiar site for the residents of the Fairway Apartments. Most of them would give me a wide berth as I went from my front door to my car. But some would stop us, so they could give him a little pat. We ran into no one that afternoon.

When I pulled up in front of the doctor's office, I turned to Parthur. "Now, you wait here." I slipped out of the car and ran up the steps to the front

Parthur

door of the vet's office. As I entered the large waiting room, Dr. Wright was just stepping out of an examination room and had just finished with his last patient of the day, a large Irish setter. The happy, long-haired, red dog was pulling on his leash and dragging his master toward the door as I approached the vet. The dog had a shaved area on his front right shoulder where I could see stitches. They exited quickly.

"I'm the one who called you about the bobcat," I stated as I held out my hand for a handshake with the vet. "I'm Dawn Fritz."

"Well, I must say, this is a first for me. A bobcat?" He was a tall, thin man, about forty-five, and with a receding hairline. He had a pair of small half glasses that perched on the end of his rather long nose. He was an absolute caricature of Ichabod Crane. "Is he in your car?"

"Yes," I replied. "I could bring him in; since you don't seem to have any other patients right now. He really is very harmless."

"No. No, that's all right," Dr. Wright quickly replied. "I'll go outside and take a look at him in your car."

The doctor and I walked out of his office and approached my car. Parthur was standing on the back of the front passenger seat. When he saw the two of us approach, his little tail started its usual action as he began to jump from the front seat to the back and to the front again. The doctor stopped and watched him. "Is he always this active?" he asked.

"Well, he thinks we are going for another drive," I offered. "He loves to ride in the car."

The vet walked around the small car, making his assessment of the bouncing animal within. "He really does have a lot of energy." He stopped and watched the energetic animal. "And you say he is quite harmless?"

"Well, if he detects you might be afraid of him, he will sometimes show aggression but he's never hurt anyone," I quickly added. I knew my beloved pet was growing up fast but his aggression to some people was a worry to me. I couldn't imagine he would ever hurt anyone, though.

"I would like to feel his muscular development and weight if you think that it is safe and possible," the doctor asked. "Maybe if you get in the car beside him and hold him, I could reach through the window and do my examination."

"Sure, that will work." I moved to the driver's side of my vehicle, opened the door and slipped behind the wheel. Parthur stopped his jumping, slipped down to the front passenger seat and looked over at me expectantly. I stroked the animal on his back to calm him as he sat back on his haunches. Then I reached across him and rolled down the passenger window. Parthur looked up at the kindly doctor and seemed to sense this was something new. This man was not a threat and he showed no fear. I put my hands around his two front legs to steady him and nodded up to the doctor. "He'll be fine now. You can go ahead and examine him."

Dr. Wright carefully reached in the car window and placed his hands on the animal's head. He patted Parthur gently and the bobcat responded by closing his eyes and sitting very still. The doctor smiled. He moved his hands down Parthur's body and felt his strong, young muscles and bones.

It was a quick exam but it was thorough. When the doctor was finished, I rolled up the window and slipped out of the car. The doctor and I walked back to his office. Parthur jumped up to the back of the front seat again to watch where we were going.

"He appears to be in excellent health," the doctor said. "In fact, he is quite a beautiful and large specimen of his breed. What have you been feeding him?" I explained that his favorite food was chicken, but he ate some beef as well. "With all that energy, though, he is not going to like being caged up for the long flight back to Illinois." We reached the front door of his office and walked in.

"I know," I answered. "That really bothers me."

Dr. Wright walked to his desk and sat behind it while I stood in front. "I've got some pills I can give you that will sedate him for several hours. They will put him into a drugged sleep that might make the trip a little more bearable for him."

"That would be great. How do I give them to him?"

"You said he liked chicken?"

"Yes," I answered, emphatically.

Dr. Wright opened a side drawer at his desk. He took out a small brown bottle and shook two pills into his hand. He then placed the two white round pills in a small tan envelope and handed them to me. "Well, crush up these two into a meal about a couple of hours before the flight. That should do the job."

"Dr. Wright, I just can't thank you enough for seeing us. What do I owe you for this very unconventional office visit?"

"No charge," he answered.

"No charge? What do you mean, no charge?"

"Look, Dawn, you've got your hands full here. That little cat was darn lucky you happened along in its life and adopted him when you did. Your problems and responsibilities have just begun. So, this one is on me."

"But, Doctor..." I protested.

"No 'buts' about it." The vet ushered me out of his office door while I was still protesting. He stood on the porch of his office as I returned to my car. "Good luck to you, Dawn," he called after me. "You're going to need it," he said under his breath.

I waved at him as I was about to get into my car. "Thanks again, Dr. Wright. I'll call you and let you know how he did on his trip. Thank you so very much." I got into my car, started up the engine and slowly backed out of the driveway. Parthur immediately took up his position on the back of the driver's seat with his body pushed up against the back of my head.

Dr. Wright smiled and shook his head as he stood on his porch and watched the little car with the two of us turn into traffic.

Parthur

Chapter 14

I purchased a large traveling kennel Parthur would use for his flight from Arizona to Illinois. It was made of beige plastic and had a metal cage door at the front. When I lugged it home to our apartment, I left it in the middle of the living room with the door of the kennel wide open. Parthur at first sniffed it suspiciously and walked around and around it. For several hours on the first day of the cage's arrival, the young cat toyed with this new, strange plaything. He hopped on top, then off, then on top again. Finally, he tentatively walked in the door. He backed out quickly. Then he walked in again. When he got used to this strange, new 'cave', he decided it was a great place to lurk and hide. Several times he ambushed

Berle and me as we walked by unsuspecting. One afternoon he even took his favorite toy, the beloved teddy bear, into the cage and took a long nap. I was pleased he seemed to have no fear of the cage and was quite comfortable with it for the time being.

My dad and I had talked several times about Parthur's airplane trip to Illinois. It was decided the last Saturday of April would be his departure date from the Phoenix airport. It certainly was not a day to which I was looking forward. I had gotten attached to my furry pet and I knew the separation was not going to be an easy one for me. Parthur's affection for me seemed just as strong, only he was unaware I would be sending him away. Berle and I were the only family Parthur could remember. I spent as much time as I could in those last few days, just sitting next to Parthur and stroking his body and scratching that right ear. Parthur loved the extra attention and would stretch and turn over on his back so I could rub his tummy. I always was delighted when Parthur would lie on his back and expose the distinctive coloring on his underside. The light-colored fur had dark spots randomly spaced on his tummy. It reminded me of un-baked chocolate chip cookie dough.

One evening, while the two of us were sitting on the couch with Parthur's body half on my lap, I reflected back to the first night I had brought him home as a small kitten. He certainly wasn't small anymore. I didn't want to face, physically, he was turning into a beautiful, mature, male bobcat. I could feel the sleek muscles under his fur, especially in his hindquarters. His face had the streaks of an adult bobcat, with long whiskers and distinctive black, gold and white striping around his eyes. The little black and white tufts of fur on the ends of his ears were now more pronounced.

When I carried Parthur to and from the apartment to my car for drives, I was noticing a major weight gain, as well. I had seen many pictures of bobcats in books and encyclopedias where the animals looked very streamlined and compact, not really a very big animal. None of those pictures of wild bobcats looked like my Parthur. My pet was not fat but he was big. He really was a beautiful and extraordinary specimen of his breed. I guess all that raw meat from Harry's meat market must have made the difference.

On the Friday before Parthur's Saturday departure, my plan was to leave for Phoenix right after I finished my last class at Kofa High. When I arrived at school on that Friday morning, Amy Stanton, one of the members of my "golf team" was waiting for me at my classroom door.

"Hi, Miss Fritz."

"Hi, Amy. It's good to see you"

"So, today is the big day for Parthur's plane ride?" My golf team had kept up with Parthur's progress all year. They felt a special bond because they were with me the night I brought him home but Amy had a special soft spot for animals. She seemed to always pay more attention to what Parthur was doing than the other girls and would continually ask questions about him when she saw me.

"Well, we leave for Phoenix tonight but he doesn't fly out until tomorrow morning."

"Aren't you going to miss him, Miss Fritz?" Amy asked.

"Probably more than I want to admit." I unlocked the door to my classroom and Amy and I walked into the empty room. "I've gotten so used to him always being there in the apartment and all the funny and crazy things he does." I paused for a minute. "But I have to look on the bright side. It will only be five weeks before I am back in Illinois, and we will be together again."

"I'm sure he will miss you, too," Amy said. "I never will forget that night we picked him up in Gila Bend. He was so little and cute but he sure has gotten bigger. When I saw him in your car last week, I couldn't believe how much he had grown."

"You're right," I said. "Like all babies, he is growing fast." Suddenly the morning bell rang, signaling students they had just ten minutes to get to their first-period class.

"See you later, Miss Fritz," Amy said and she left the classroom as my first-period students started swarming in the door.

I reflected for a moment. "I wonder just what problems do lay ahead when Parthur is full grown?" Well, I couldn't spend a lot of time worrying about that right now. Tomorrow, Parthur had a plane to catch and tonight I had to get the two of us to Phoenix.

Chapter 15

At the end of the school day, I hurried home to our apartment. Parthur, as usual, was eagerly awaiting my arrival as he watched for me at the front window from his table. Of course, he wanted to play. While I hurriedly packed my small overnight bag, I threw a ball for him a couple of times.

Parthur soon lost interest in the ball and decided to see what I was doing. He watched with great interest as I closed the large traveling kennel that had been sitting in the middle of the living room and struggled with it out the front door. He jumped to his window table and watched me as I passed in front of his picture window and then turned the corner, leading out to the car port.

When I came back into the apartment, he jumped off his perch and sat on the kitchen floor and studied me as I was getting together items and placing them on the kitchen table. His long thin tongue licked his lips as he watched me pull chicken from the refrigerator and wrap it in wax paper. I added it to the pile. Then I placed all the items on the table in a small cooler with two cans of soda and a bag of ice. Parthur loved the taste of soda. I'd never let him have very much, but when I would put a little in a saucer for him, it would make his nose tingle.

I made several more trips out the front door of the apartment to my car. Parthur again sat on the small table at the window and watched me go in and out. When I took his beloved teddy bear out the door, Parthur became a little anxious but when I came back and picked him up and started for the front door, he knew he was going for a ride.

The drive to Phoenix was the longest trip Parthur could remember. He was used to small trips around Yuma so he soon lost interest in looking out the window from his perch on the back of the driver's seat behind my head. The sound of the engine's motor made him sleepy and he curled up on the passenger's seat and took a long nap.

I looked over at him with affection often. I knew it was going to be tough to say goodbye tomorrow at the airport.

It was early evening by the time I reached Phoenix. The sky was a clear, dark blue toward the east with a few stars peeking out on the far horizon, but there was still a little light to the west. I made my way to the area around the Phoenix Sky Harbor Airport where I knew there were many motels. I spotted a Holiday Inn sign and pulled in. I drove slowly past the office, where I saw a young woman behind the registration desk then I parked my car up against a large hedge down from the office entrance, where it was quite dark. Hopefully out of view of the front desk.

Parthur was wide awake now and was jumping from the front seat to the back seat, trying to get a better view of these new surroundings.

I rolled down my window and leaned out to see if the registration clerk could see my car. I was satisfied it was just out of her view. I decided it just wasn't necessary to let the hotel personnel see my exotic and frisky pet and start to ask questions. I quickly turned off the head lights of my little car.

"Parthur, you be still now," I scolded the excited animal as I prepared to leave the car. Parthur just looked at me expectantly as he stood on all fours in the front seat. I rolled up the window and slipped out of the car door and walked up to the motel office, while the young cat watched me from the rear window of the car.

"Hi," said the young woman behind the registration desk. "Welcome to the Holiday Inn. Can I help you?"

"Sure, "I said. "I need a single room for one night." I hesitated. "Listen, I am a very light sleeper. Is there any way you could put me on the first floor and down on a quiet end?" I felt a little guilty about lying but I didn't think I wanted to advertise Parthur's presence.

"No problem," the receptionist answered. "We're not real busy tonight. I'll put you down on the end of this building. Will that be all right?"

"Perfect," I answered. I filled out the registration form and quickly returned to my car. With a room key bearing the number 126, I slowly drove down to the far end of the large, white, two-story building. I parked right in front of the door marked 126. I sat there for a few minutes and looked back and forth. No one seemed to be around. I clutched my room key in my left hand, opened the car door and leaned over and picked up Parthur. Quickly, I was at the motel room door, had it unlocked and was in the room with my animal. I was quite certain no one had seen us. I dropped Parthur in the middle of the big king-size bed with a sigh of relief then went back to the car to get the rest of our things.

Parthur loved the motel room with all its new smells and was not satisfied until he had sniffed out every corner of the bedroom and the bathroom. While he was checking everything out, I arranged my overnight things and opened the cooler for a soda. I even had a small sandbox for Parthur, and I placed it in the bathroom for him. We were set for the evening.

I fixed our dinner. I had a sandwich for myself with a bag of chips and a soda, and Parthur had half a chicken. He attacked his meal with a ravenous gusto, gnawing up everything. After we ate, I decided to take a shower before I went to bed. The shower in our apartment back in Yuma had a shower door on it, but here at the Holiday Inn there was a tub with a shower curtain. While I was standing in the tub washing my hair, I saw the curtain move. Before I could stop him, and before he could stop himself, Parthur slid into the bathtub with me. "Parthur," I scolded.

Parthur

He didn't like the hard spray of water from the shower head or the soapy suds in the tub. All he wanted was to get out. The slippery conditions were making it difficult but, finally, with my help and a great deal of splashing, he was out of the tub. His fur was soaked and a big puddle of water was forming under him on the bathroom floor. He shook himself once, trying to rid himself of all the water then he shook himself again. He flicked each leg independently and finally walked out of the bathroom, indignantly leaving a huge wet mess.

Parthur was still a little damp by the time I had finished my shower and had cleaned up his mess, but he was busily washing himself down with his rough tongue. I used one of the motel's big towels and wrapped Parthur up in it and carried him to the large bed. I encircled my arms around the terry-cloth bundle to help him get completely dry. Parthur was appreciative of the towel's warmth and my attention. He hated being wet.

Later, after dressing for bed and Parthur was completely dry, I turned on the small television set at the end of the bed and got under the covers after I arranged the pillows for better television viewing.

Parthur sensed there was something wrong with me, I seemed sad. I was showering him with attention but something told him there was going to be a change. He sat down next to me with his body pushed up against my hip. I stroked the soft fur of his back and then moved my hand up to his ears and started scratching. When I got to the right ear, Parthur pushed toward me and stretched. I smiled then I gave him the 'thumbs up' sign. Parthur looked at me and obliged. Tap, tap, tap went his right paw. He even would give the sign if he was lying down. I laughed out loud and ruffled the fur on the top of his head.

It took me a long time to fall asleep that night but finally I did get a few fitful hours. I kept dreaming the same dream over and over. It was always about Parthur. In my dream I had lost him and couldn't find him. Each time I awoke, I would reach out to see if Parthur was still there. He never moved from my side all night.

Then it was morning.

Parthur

Chapter 16

The scheduled flight Parthur was to take left the Phoenix Airport at 9:30 in the morning. I was up at 6:30, and quickly got dressed. I packed up all my belongings and placed them next to the door of my motel room. At seven-thirty, I fed Parthur the chicken I had kept out. I smashed the two pills that Dr. Wright had given me and rubbed the white powder into the chicken meat. Parthur devoured his breakfast. If the pills gave an added flavor, he certainly didn't seem to mind. He always had a great appetite.

It was time to leave. I gently pushed back the curtains on the window of the motel room and peeked out into the parking lot to see if there was anyone out there. Just to my right I could see the pushcart of a cleaning woman from the hotel but there was no one in sight next to the cart or in the parking lot. I quickly carried my packed belongings out of the room to the car. Coming back, I looked around and saw the door to the room next to mine was open. I could see the maid making the bed with her back to me. The maid never turned around or looked up. Quickly, I opened the door to my room and grabbed Parthur. Clutching him to my chest, I raced through the door and jumped into my car. I looked back at the cleaning lady. She was still hard at work on the bed and had not taken notice of us. I started up my car and drove down to the registration office at the end of the building. Once again, I parked my car out of view of the office front desk. I went in, paid my bill then left for the airport.

I arrived at the front of the Package Express Office of United Airlines at 8 o'clock. My car was the only one there. Parthur was curled up in the front passenger's seat. It appeared that the pills might already be working. I reached over and patted him on his head and Parthur responded with a little stretch and a yawn. I got out of my car and removed the large traveling kennel from the back seat of the car. I lugged the big empty cage into the office and, as I entered, a baggage handler motioned for me to place it on a low shelf that served as a scale.

"You sending a pet?" the baggage handler asked me.

"Yes."

"Where to?"

"Moline, Illinois."

"Fill out these papers and then bring in your pet. We'll have to weigh the cage with him in it." He handed me some documents and then turned and busied himself with other paperwork.

"All right." It took me almost ten minutes but finally all the papers were completed. I handed them back to the baggage handler.

He absently looked over the pages. "Well, bring in your pet," he said. I was pretty certain he hadn't paid any attention to the line in the paperwork that had asked the kind of animal I was sending. I walked out of the office to retrieve Parthur.

I walked slowly back to the car. When I opened the passenger-side door, Parthur didn't even move. He was curled up in a deep sleep. *Dr. Wright's pills are definitely working*, I thought. I reached down and picked up the sleeping animal. His body felt slack in my arms and his eyes were only half open. He was making a soft, rattling purring sound that brought a smile to my face. I gently and slowly walked back into the baggage handling office with the drugged animal.

The baggage handler looked up as I re-entered the office. "Whoa, wait a minute, lady. That's a wild animal." He backed up against the wall with his hands held up protectively in front of his chest.

"Don't worry. He won't hurt you," I assured him.

The man looked terrified and watched my every move as he backed even further away from me to a corner of the office. "I'll just wait over here until you get him in that cage."

I stood in front of the traveling kennel. I just didn't want to part with my pet and place him inside. I hugged him to my chest. Finally, I sat down next to the cage, cradling the sleeping animal in my arms and petted him over and over. The baggage handler stood frozen in the corner of the office. "You'll love my dad and mom," I whispered to Parthur, as a tear slid down my cheek. "And it won't be long before I'm back in Illinois with you." I sat in silence for just a moment more. "Please be good." The two of us sat there for a few more minutes in silence. Then, finally, I placed the drowsy animal in the cage and slowly closed the door. I looked through the wire bars of the cage door. He looked so peaceful. I wiped a tear from my cheek. I looked up at the attendant. He had been watching me carefully. He noted the weight of the kennel with Parthur in and gave me the bill. I paid him in cash and turned to leave the building.

When I reached the door of the office, I suddenly remembered something. "Wait a minute. Don't load him yet. I've left something of his in the car." The baggage handler watched me rush out the door to my car. He was still standing in the same place when I returned with Parthur's beloved teddy bear. I rushed back to the cage, opened the cage door and carefully placed the stuffed animal next to the sleeping cat. Parthur lifted his head with his eyes half closed; when he smelled its presence he put one of his front paws over it protectively. Immediately he was asleep again. "Goodbye," I whispered as I slowly and carefully closed the cage door again. I then turned to the baggage handler, "You will take good care of him, won't you?"

"Yes, lady," he nodded. "We'll take good care of him." From a drawer he had pulled out some long, thick work gloves and was putting them on as I slowly left the office.

Parthur

The long drive back to Yuma was a sad one. There were tears, there were doubts I was doing the right thing then there were more tears. There was such emptiness in the car then I cried again. I knew my dad and mom would take good care of Parthur but, wow, was I ever going to miss him.

When I got back to Yuma, I stayed by the phone waiting to hear from my parents. I wanted to make sure Parthur had arrived safely. Berle had left around 6 o'clock with a group of our friends to go out to dinner and see a movie. "Are you sure you won't go with us?" she had asked.

"No, I have to know he made it safely."

Berle understood.

It was late that evening when the phone finally rang. I jumped to answer it. "He's here," my dad said, "and he's in great shape."

"Oh, Dad, I have been so worried."

"He made a big hit at the Quad City Airport," he went on. "Someone must have called ahead, because all the baggage handlers were wearing big thick gloves."

"How was he acting?" I asked. "Was he showing any signs of aggression?" My dad and I had talked about some of the incidents where Parthur had been aggressive to people who showed fear.

"No, he really was pretty docile but he could hardly wait to get out of that cage. I remembered you told me how he loved to ride in cars. So, as soon as your mom and I could, we turned him loose in the car. He loved it. And was he ever hungry. The first thing we did when we got back to Hawthorn Hill was to give him some chicken like you said. We gave him a whole one and he devoured it." Dad went on and on about Parthur's arrival in Illinois. The young cat seemed to have made the trip to the Midwest with little or no difficulties. I sighed in relief.

"Remember, Dad, he loves to be scratched behind his ears, especially the right one."

"We've already done that, Dawn. We'll take good care of him. Don't you worry. And, I'm glad you sent him with his teddy bear. He takes it with him everywhere he goes."

I hoped it made Parthur think of me. I smiled.

Chapter 17

Parthur loved it at Hawthorn Hill. The sprawling log cabin home of Bee and Ken Fritz was nestled on top of a high hill overlooking the Mississippi River and it backed up to a thick wood. Parthur's first night in Illinois was spent exploring every inch of his new home. It was fascinating to the young animal with all its new smells. His favorite place was the large wrap-around porch that covered two sides of the home. It had screens that went from floor to ceiling and allowed the young bobcat great views of his surroundings. On one side he could see the flickering waters of the Mississippi River down over the front hill. On the other side he could look into the back yard that abutted up to a thick wood that looked dense and inviting. Whichever way the wind shifted, from the river side or from the woods, Parthur could sit for hours drinking in their special odors. It seemed like every day he had a new smell to contemplate. He always kept his teddy bear near.

There was only one thing he didn't like at Hawthorn Hill, and that was Ken's two fox hounds named Brutus and Caesar. Bee was a Latin and English teacher at a near-by farming community's high school, Orion, hence the Roman names. When Parthur first arrived and the dogs had spotted him for the first time on the screened porch, there had been a lot of howling, barking and growling. They made aggressive lunges at him with Ken intervening as best he could. The porch screens kept the dogs and cat separated. Ken never allowed the dogs in the house, but when they were outside and within sight of the cat on the screened porch, the hounds always made it very clear they did not like the presence of Parthur. The feeling was mutual.

The dogs, however, were easily intimidated by Parthur. They were not the smartest of their breed, and the young bobcat would hold his ground, growl, hiss and bat at the dogs on his side of the screen. As the days rolled by, the dogs, for the most part, ignored him. Every now and then though, when one of the hounds saw him on the porch, it would voice, from afar, a long low howl to show its opposition to his presence but, mostly, they gave the screened porch a wide berth. They were not at all happy he shared Hawthorn Hill with them. By the end of May, Parthur had settled into the Fritz's routines. He missed Dawn a lot and kept looking for her around the house, hoping she would turn up but he accepted

Parthur

Bee and Ken into his life. They lavished lots of attention on him and he liked that. Parthur had always slept on the end of Dawn's bed in Yuma but, here at Hawthorn Hill, he chose a small couch on the woods side of the screened porch as his sleeping place. He had thought about jumping up on Ken and Bee's bed on one of the first nights he was there but it just wasn't the same.

The nights were getting warmer and Parthur loved to listen to all the night sounds from the woods that grew so close to the log-cabin home. He used to sleep soundly through the night at Dawn's apartment, but now he spent many of his nights walking back and forth on the big, screened-in porch, looking out into the night and listening and watching. Wild bobcats are nocturnal by nature and he was falling into that pattern.

One night, just after Ken and Bee had gone to bed, Parthur jumped down from his sleeping couch, began pacing back and forth on the large porch, looking out into the night and breathing in its smells. He stopped his pacing and walked into the kitchen to his water dish for a drink. After he quenched his thirst, he wandered over to the screen door to the back porch and looked out. It was a mild night and this was the first time Parthur had found the back door open with just the screen door between him and the outdoors. For some reason, he pushed up against the screen door with his nose and was surprised to find that it gave a little. Someone had forgotten to hook the latch. He pushed on it again, and it opened a couple of inches. Then he gave it a mighty push with his front shoulder, and he was standing on the little back porch in the moonlight. The screen door closed behind him with a soft thump.

Parthur stood there for a moment, looked at the closed screen door and then walked over and peered over the railing into the yard below. The porch was almost twelve feet high above the ground with steps off to one side, leading down into the back area of the yard. He looked back at the closed screen door he had just opened then he looked down at the back yard and out into the woods. He had very distant memories of the cave where he was born but this was so fascinating. It didn't take long, however, for his curiosity to make the decision to head out into the night. He quickly walked down the steep steps of the porch and headed for the large flower bed in the back of the yard.

He had watched Bee plant various green plants there just that afternoon. He shoved his nose in amongst the new vegetation. The dirt smelled musty and moist where she had been digging. He pawed at the newly turned garden, lowered his nose into it again and took some large, deep breaths of the loamy earth. Some of the dirt stuck to his nose and tickled him. He sneezed it out with a soft cough.

He then decided to investigate more; he loved all this new freedom. He trotted over to the front yard, which was the highest point of Hawthorn Hill. He sat down and surveyed all that was spread out in front of him. From there he could look out over the dark, wide, Mississippi River spread out below him at the bottom of the hill as a giant ink spill. The moon's glow made a splintered path across its middle. A light breeze was blowing up the hill from the river and the young cat closed his eyes and

Parthur pushed his nose into the air to enjoy all the wonderful river smells: fish, algae, birds, dampness, moss, mold, plants.

He sat there motionless for some time, enjoying the night, when he noticed a small movement out of the corner of his eye. He didn't move but his body was alert and his round, yellow eyes swiveled as they focused and watched closely for whatever it was. Slowly, a little mouse made its zigzagging way across the lawn about six feet from where the cat sat. Parthur watched it without moving as it approached him, getting closer and closer. The little mouse, not knowing a huge feline was near its path, stopped and started several times. Finally, it was within three feet of the still cat. Parthur's instincts took over and he pounced on the small animal, trapping him under his two oversized, front paws.

The mouse struggled and Parthur lifted one paw to let him partially escape. The terrified mouse pulled himself loose from under Parthur's other paw and gained its freedom but just as the mouse was about to bound away, Parthur pounced on him again. For half an hour Parthur played the 'catch and escape' game with the frantic mouse. Finally, the exhausted small animal wouldn't move anymore. He had given up and had accepted his fate. Parthur prodded it with a soft paw several times to get it to move. The cat was gentle, investigative and careful. Parthur than began to lick the petrified creature until it was completely covered with wet saliva from its pointed nose to its tail. The mouse never made an attempt to move. Parthur looked down at the tiny, wet, motionless creature that was sprawled on its back, pawed at him one more time and then decided to let it go.

The mouse lay still for several minutes, waiting for whatever was going to happen to it next. Slowly, it dawned on it that it might live and its tormentor might let him go. He righted himself, moved carefully and then waited to see what the cat would do. The cat did not move. The mouse weakly and slowly crawled away. Parthur watched closely as the exhausted mouse took cover in some weeds nearby.

Parthur turned his back on the river and trotted into the back yard and headed straight into the deep woods that hugged the edge of Bee's flower garden. He easily navigated the dense underbrush where the light of the moon could hardly penetrate. His sharp cat's eyes adjusted to the dark as his pupils grew round and expanded to almost fill his entire eye socket. He trotted softly and silently away from the Fritz's log home.

The smells were wonderful. There were so many things to sniff and touch with his soft wet nose, but he didn't stop. He traveled deeper and deeper into the woods. Suddenly, he stopped at the base of a huge elm tree. Three morel mushrooms had poked their sponge like heads up from the decayed leaves and grasses. He sniffed at them and then stood on his hind legs and sharpened his claws on the rough bark of the tree's trunk. Small shards of elm bark fell around him. He dropped down from the sharpening, turned and looked back in the direction he had come. He hesitated but, after a few minutes, he continued on with his quick trot deeper into the woods until he arrived at a small meadow partially carpeted with a thick, deep moss. The moon shone down here making his eyes shine as blue-green jewels. And then, he began to jump like a fawn. He pranced and jumped in a dizzying dance in the small glade for over fifteen minutes. Then, suddenly, he stopped and he looked over his shoulder and hesitated. He stood there for some time then he turned around and headed back the way he had come; back towards Hawthorn Hill.

He broke free of the underbrush and was once more in the backyard of the Fritz home. He stopped and hesitated. He looked over his shoulder, peering back into the woods. He looked back at the big log house that stood dark and black against the night sky. His tail twitched several times then he moved toward the home.

Now he decided to walk around the house, since he really had only investigated two sides of it so far. He took his time as he searched out all the corners and flower beds along the way. He smelled the smell of the two hound dogs in a lot of the areas of the yard. Their scents were most intense at the outside basement door. He growled a low menacing growl at their smell that surprised him. It was the protective growl of the wild he had never used before yet he was having too much fun exploring all these wonderful new things to give much thought to those pesky dogs. Besides, he sensed they were of no threat to him this night because they were locked in the basement.

When Parthur reached the back yard again he investigated the thick blanket of trees and underbrush making up the perimeter of the woods. He ducked back into its dark protective comfort. He started off at a slow trot away from the back yard. Suddenly he stopped, hesitated, turned and headed back. He hadn't penetrated the woods this time as deeply as before and he certainly hadn't stayed very long.

Just as he exited the woods for the second time, the eastern sky was starting to get light; signaling the beginning of the new day. Parthur was aware of the Fritz's schedules. They were early risers. Bee Fritz was always the first one into the kitchen. Parthur's stomach told him it was almost his breakfast time, so he turned away from his explorations and headed back to the back porch. He climbed up the steep stairs to the back porch and sat down in front of the closed screen door; waiting for Bee. He was sitting there looking in when Bee walked into the kitchen.

"Parthur." she exclaimed. "What are you doing out there?" She then saw the hook was dangling on the screened door and knew it had not been locked the night before. She surmised the cat must have pushed his way out. Quickly, she opened the door and Parthur sauntered in. "Oh, Parthur, we would have hated to have lost you. I'm glad you stayed close to home." She kept talking to the cat while she fixed his breakfast and, every now and then, she reached down to pat his head. "I wonder what you did all night and where you went. Dawn will be here in only two weeks. If you had run away, she would have been so unhappy."

Parthur liked to listen to her voice. When his breakfast was finished, he walked out onto the front porch and jumped up into his special chair. He took a long nap and dreamed about all the things he had seen and smelled the night before.

Parthur

Chapter 18

In Yuma, the month of May couldn't pass fast enough for me. Berle's seven-week-old Chihuahua arrived two days after Parthur flew to Illinois but the little puppy just could not fill the emptiness for me that Parthur had left in the apartment. Berle called the little dog "Twitch" because he always looked as if he were shivering. He had very little hair on his body, and he always appeared to be cold. In those early weeks the little Chihuahua liked to stay wrapped up in a blanket and be held. I missed all the roughhouse play and action of Parthur.

Parthur's table still remained in the front window of our apartment and I could not break the habit of always looking for my pet in the window as I arrived home from school each day. Finally, one afternoon, I pulled it back away from the big picture window and positioned it next to the couch.

Fortunately, the year-end activities at Kofa High School kept me involved and busy. The close of the school year brought papers to be corrected, students to be counseled, meetings and exams. My yearbook class had received the "annuals" and that meant distribution to the whole school. I was glad my days were filled with activities. I was counting the days, however, 'til the end of the school year because then I would be able to leave for Illinois.

Finally, that day arrived, and I loaded up my little car and headed home to Hawthorn Hill. I drove east on Highway 80 and smiled as I passed through Gila Bend and saw the small restaurant where I had met Nancy Copeland. It seemed just yesterday I and my "golf team" had stopped there for breakfast. It was hard to believe Parthur had been a part of my life for only eight months. I thought about stopping to see if Nancy was still at the restaurant. I was sure she would have liked an update on Parthur, but I was in too much of a hurry to get back home to Illinois. I keep pushing east.

After two and a half days of driving, I arrived back at Hawthorn Hill late in the afternoon. I was so excited as my little car made its way up the winding gravel road that led to the top of the hill and my parents' home. Would Parthur remember me? I jumped out of the car and raced up the back steps and into the kitchen. My mom was at the stove fixing dinner and Parthur was sitting on a small braided rug in front of the sink. He heard the footsteps coming up to the steps to the back door and stood up when I walked in. I knelt in the doorway as the animal eyed me. I held out my hand then gave the 'thumbs up' sign. Parthur instinctively patted that right front foot three times; tap, tap, tap.

It took the cat only a couple of seconds to realize it was me and he rushed into my arms. He rolled and pushed up against me and he licked my arms and face. I sat with him in the middle of the kitchen floor for over an hour. Each time I tried to get up, he would push up against me again so I would lose my balance and have to stay on the floor with him. My mom and I laughed at his insistence on being so close. Parthur would not let me move away from him. It was almost as if he feared if I left his side, he would never see me again. I hugged him and held him in my lap.

"Parthur, I'm going to have to get up sooner or later," I said to the cat, as I stroked his back and scratched his ears. Finally, I was able to extract myself from the young animal but he stayed by my side wherever I went. When I went back to my car to unload my things, he stood anxiously by the back door waiting for me to return with that small tail of his switching back and forth.

For the next two days Parthur wouldn't let me out of his sight. Several times I almost tripped over him because he stayed so close to my feet. "I think he just wants to make sure I don't leave him again," I told my parents.

Chapter 19

Things finally settled down to a normal routine at Hawthorn Hill. About two weeks after I arrived home, I received a phone call from the local newspaper, the *Moline Daily Dispatch*. Someone had told them the Fritz family had a pet bobcat and the newspaper wanted to send out a reporter and a photographer to do a story on him. I was a little hesitant but the young woman on the phone was insistent and finally persuaded me to do it. When I got off the phone, I turned to Parthur and said, "You're going to be famous."

The newspaper reporter, Les Adams, and his photographer, Bob Griffen, arrived two days later on a bright, sunny morning. Parthur heard their knock at the front door and rushed to see who was there. As I ushered the two men out onto the wide, screened porch, Parthur made a mock attack at the photographer's pant leg, wrapped his front paws around one of his ankles and hung on. The photographer stopped, frozen in terror, clutching his equipment to his chest. "Parthur," I scolded. "Don't do that to that poor man." I reached down and extracted the young animal from around Bob's leg. He wasn't hurt but now the man was terrified of Parthur and the bobcat knew and sensed it. Parthur's little tail whipped back and forth as he sized up the photographer. He felt his fear and his sharp eyes sparkled with mischief. "I'm sorry," I said to the two men. "He really is just playing with you. He won't hurt you." The photographer was not convinced.

Les, Bob and I all moved to one end of the front porch. Parthur had slipped behind a couch and Bob was frantically trying to locate him as he set up his cameras. Les and I sat at a long wooden, dinner table made of bleached half logs and he began his interview.

"Does he always attack guests?" Les asked.

"No, not really," I replied. "When he thinks he has someone on the defense and a little intimidated, he won't give up, however. He's like a bad child picking on a weaker kid." Secretly, I wondered about these attacks. Was Parthur showing an aggressive side that could ever be a problem for me or my family? I shook those thoughts from my mind. I just would not believe my warm, lovable pet could ever hurt us or anyone else.

Suddenly, there was a terrified yelp from Bob. Les and I turned to look. Parthur had just made another pass at him from behind the couch. The cat had darted out from his hiding place, batted Bob's ankles then had run into the other room. Obviously, the young cat was having a great time but Bob wasn't.

"He really is just playing with you," I told Bob again.

He looked miserable but he smiled weakly at me, trying to believe he was not in danger. For Bob's sake, Les made the interview with me as short as he could. Bob couldn't wait to leave Hawthorn Hill and Parthur but in spite of his fears, he got some great photos of the cat and me. They appeared a few days later in the *Dispatch*.

After the feature-length article appeared in the newspaper, I received a call from the Quad City Wild Animal Farm, which had just recently opened its gates in Moline. They had put together an impressive display of wild animals that included many of the big wild cats. They were interested in my bobcat.

"Parthur is not available for your wild animal farm," I firmly told Jeff Long, the head ranger. "He's my pet."

"Could I just come and see him?"

"You are wasting your time," I hotly told him. "Why would you just want to come and look at him if he is not available?"

"Look, Dawn, the wild cats are my favorites. I studied them in college and they have always intrigued me. Please, won't you just let me come and see your animal?" Jeff was insistent and he finally convinced me to allow him to visit Parthur the next day.

Jeff arrived in the late afternoon. He was a tall, fit man in his late thirties and it was obvious he had a soft and gentle way with animals. Parthur liked him immediately when he met him as he entered the back door. The ranger leaned down, patted the cat on his head and scratched him behind the ears. I ushered Jeff out to the front porch and Parthur followed. The ranger and I sat at the same bleached, half log, dinner table and talked as Parthur bounded to and fro after imaginary objects. Several times when he stopped by me for some attention, he eyed Jeff but then he would dash off on some imaginary mission.

The ranger watched him with close interest. "What a beautiful animal you have, Dawn. He is of extraordinary size." He paused. "You know you have your hands full?"

I nodded.

"I can tell he cares for you a great deal but his personality can change dramatically when he reaches full maturity. He is going to need a mate. When he can't find one he may get anxious. This could be a problem for you and your family. By his size, I don't think that's far off. How old is he?" the ranger asked.

"He was born in October, so he's a few months away from being a year old."

"I thought as much," Jeff said. "We just received some information the other day about another pet bobcat like yours in the area. He had been a loving pet for over a year. Then one day he turned on his family, without any warning."

I listened closely but I said nothing.

Jeff continued, "Bobcats have very strong hind leg muscles. This particular bobcat jumped on the back of the father and really did some damage with his hind claws. The man had to be hospitalized and the animal had to be destroyed. I would hate to see that happen to anyone in your family or to your pet."

"Parthur wouldn't do that," I retorted, quickly. "He loves all of us." I hated to admit what the ranger was saying did make sense. I had noticed several little changes in Parthur upon my return. He was a lot more independent now than he had been back in Yuma but surely, my family and I were safe from any attack from him.

The ranger went on, "I know how you feel about him and I can see how Parthur feels about you. You are going to have to face reality, though. Bobcats are one of the smaller animals among the wild felines but they can be dangerous." He paused. "You could have the animal neutered. That might take care of any aggressive problems. There is no guarantee, though."

I remembered that Dr. Hibben's pet bobcat back at the University of New Mexico had been neutered. Somehow, I just didn't want to do that. "I'd really hate to do that to him," I replied. "I was just hoping things would work out. I guess maybe I'm being just a little naive."

"Dawn, I can see you love Parthur and you want to do the right thing. Your constant handling and touching of him every day, I feel, is the only thing keeping him from his natural, wild instincts. I don't think you'll have many more weeks or months, though, before you start to see some really big changes in him."

I sat in silence as I listened to Jeff. I didn't want to believe what he was saying.

Jeff stood up to leave, "Keep in touch with us. You know we would love to have Parthur at our farm. I promise you; we would give him the best of care."

"But he would be behind bars," I protested. "He's never been a caged animal and I don't think I could do that to him." I watched as Parthur leapt out from behind a chair, clutching his teddy bear gently in his mouth. He placed it carefully on the floor, sat down next to it and began to give it a complete washing. The teddy bear had lost most of its fur by now and its two eyes had been missing for some time, from the constant cleanings Parthur inflicted on it with his raspy, tongue. I smiled as I watched him. "I don't think I will ever need your wild animal farm, Jeff"

After the ranger left, I sat on the couch watching Parthur taking care of his teddy bear. Was the ranger right? Would Parthur's personality change in the near future? I just couldn't imagine my family or I could ever be in any danger from my pet.

Parthur sensed I was troubled. He moved away from his cleaning job and jumped up on the couch next to me. I rubbed his head and stroked his back. Parthur curled up next to me and started to take a little nap as I sat looking out into the back woods through the large screens that half circled the house. Was I really doing the right thing?

Parthur

Chapter 20

I didn't want to admit it but Parthur was changing. When I had returned to Illinois from Arizona, Parthur had taken up his sleeping position on the end of my bed on my first night back but on the next night, when I bent down to pat him in the middle of the night, I discovered he was no longer there. I put on my slippers to see where he had gone. I tip toed trough the dark and silent house and found him on the large wrap-around porch, looking out into the woods. A soft breeze coming through the screens ruffled his fur as I sat down next to him. He looked over at me then turned and continued his steady stare into the trees bordering the back yard. I patted him on his head. "What do you see, Parthur?" I whispered.

He looked over at me again but then turned, lifted his head to fill his nostrils from the light breeze and continued to stare out into the dark. After that night, he never slept on my bed again.

By the first of August, Parthur's demeanor had changed radically. He had been such a social animal with humans since I could remember but now, that had all changed. He always had been the first one at the door whenever there was a knock but now he ignored all visitors. At mealtimes, he had always been under the dinner table and under everyone's feet moving from one member of the family to another, waiting to be stroked, scratched and petted but now he was never there. The young bobcat now spent hours off by himself. He would search out dark and secluded spots and curl up to be alone. Many times, I would hunt down his new hiding places and try to coax him out. Sometimes I was able to bring him back into the family but more and more often I was met with growls. I decided it was best to give him his space but I missed him terribly.

Parthur himself wasn't sure why he was changing. He loved the Fritz family, especially Dawn but he needed to be by himself. There was something he needed and he just wasn't sure what. His dreams were filled with the sights and sounds of his one night out at Hawthorn Hill. He was confused and chose to be by himself to think about it. He didn't like it when he growled at the family but he needed his space.

One afternoon, I walked out on the large front porch and stopped in stunned disbelief. Parthur's favorite toy, his teddy bear, was torn and ripped apart into tiny little pieces and was strewn all over the floor. I quickly went on a search for my pet. Why would he do that? It was his favorite possession and now it was ripped to shreds. I finally found him under a bed in the guest room in the farthest dark corner. I was on my knees holding up a corner of the bedspread when I spotted him.

"Parthur," I called softly. "Parthur, are you all right?" He did not make a sound.

I got down on my stomach and pushed myself under the single bed. I reached out my hand to the tightly curled-up animal. "Parthur," I called again. This time I heard a low, menacing growl but I pushed myself farther under the bed until I was close enough to reach out and softly touch his body.

He growled again and suddenly turned and snapped at me. His movement was so fast, at first, I wasn't even sure he had bitten me but one of his front fangs had caught my little finger and had ripped it open. I bumped my head on the underside of the bed as I jerked my bleeding finger back as I felt the pain. Slowly, I pushed myself out from under the bed and sat up. My finger was bleeding quite badly now, as blood rushed out of the wound. I tried to stem the flow of blood by putting pressure at the base of the torn finger with my other hand. I couldn't believe Parthur had actually bitten me.

Tears filled my eyes. They were not so much from the pain of the wound but from the realization my pet had changed. I was convinced Parthur would not really harm me and that this was just an accident but I also couldn't forget the advice and warnings Jeff Long, the ranger at the wild animal farm, had given me. Would Parthur get more aggressive in the future? Might he bite my mother or my father? I hated to be asking myself these questions but I knew I had to face the reality of the changing personality of the young bobcat.

Slowly, I stood up and walked into the bathroom to take care of my bleeding finger. As I stood at the sink, running cold water over the wound, I felt the brush of Parthur's fur against my leg. I looked down at him as he rubbed up against me again. It was almost as if he were asking to be forgiven. I dried my hands and retrieved the large, tin Band-Aid box out of the medicine cabinet. Still dripping blood, I finally managed to get two large bandages tightly affixed over the wound. Parthur sat down in the middle of the bathroom floor and watched me. When I was certain I had contained the wound, I looked at him and reached down to pat his head. I knew he had not meant to hurt me. "Parthur, what can we do?" I asked. "If only things could be like they were when you were a baby." I knew that was impossible. Parthur was a full-grown mature bobcat and his needs were different now. I had been trying for days to ignore these facts but now I would have to face them.

Parthur knew he had hurt Dawn. He couldn't believe he had bitten her, the only mother he could remember. He had been in one of those dreams again when Dawn had touched him and the snap at her hand had been a reflexive action he now wished he could take back. He rubbed her leg again.

I tried to conceal the bite from my parents but at dinner time my dad spotted the blood-soaked bandages. "What's that?" he asked.

I tried to act as if it were nothing. "Just a scratch."

Parthur

"That's not just a scratch." My dad was good with wounds and insisted I take off the bandages so he could examine it. "This is a deep wound. How did you get it?"

I couldn't lie and I told him what had happened.

"Dawn, I was afraid of this."

"Dad, I know Parthur didn't mean to hurt me."

"We have all seen the changes in him. You cannot ignore he has been turning away from all of us for some time now, even you," Dad said. "The ranger predicted that his personality might change."

"I know, I know, Dad," I answered, "but this change happened so fast. I know you told me months ago I needed to think ahead to the time when he would be a full-grown bobcat." I hesitated. "I guess the time has come."

"I know this is hard for you," Dad replied, "but you have to think about the safety of our family. Wild animals are just not meant to be house pets or any kind of pet."

"You know we all love Parthur but you must think of the consequences," Mom added.

"I don't want any of us harmed but I feel so responsible for him," I choked out. We were all sitting at the kitchen table and I lowered my face into my arms on the table. I shook my head back and forth, "Oh, why is it turning out like this?" Suddenly, I thought I felt the brush of his fur on my leg. Quickly. I lifted my face and looked expectantly under the table to see if Parthur was there at his usual spot. He wasn't. He probably had crawled off to some dark corner again.

"Your mother and I know how you feel, Dawn. We both love Parthur but I think you had better give that ranger a call," Dad said.

"Dad, they will put him in a cage. I don't know if I could stand that. I don't know if Parthur could handle that." Tears were filling my eyes. All three of us sat in silence for several minutes. None of us wanted to give up on the young bobcat that had been such a delight to all three of us but we knew something had to be done, especially me.

"Dawn, I know how you feel. I know how I feel. This will not be easy but something has to be done," Dad said.

"Dad, why can't we just turn him loose here in our back yard?"

"I'm afraid he is just not equipped, Dawn. No one has taught him how to hunt. He has no fear of humans, which could be a big problem. Then there are the dogs. There would be so many obstacles for him to overcome for him to make it on his own."

I was miserable. What my dad was saying made sense. He was right. The discussion about Parthur went on for over an hour between the three of us.

"Dawn, you will just have to call Jeff Long at the wild animal farm. It's the only answer I can see for Parthur."

I couldn't believe I was going to have to give up my pet but there didn't seem to be any other answer. Parthur didn't mean to bite me, I was certain. Maybe he would change back to the way he used to be but I knew that wouldn't happen. I kept trying to rationalize the situation but I knew what had to be done. Finally, with resignation, I said, "Dad, I'll call Jeff in the morning."

My dad got up from his chair and crossed over to me. He gave me a big hug. He knew how much Parthur meant to me. He knew how much Parthur meant to all of us. This was not an easy thing for his daughter to do and he was proud of her.

Parthur

Chapter 21

It was a long night for all three of us. None of us slept well. I turned and thrashed all night. Once, just before daybreak, I thought I felt Parthur at the end of my bed but, when I leaned down to feel for him, he was not there. I got up to look for him and, once again, I found him on the screened porch looking out into the back woods. I sat next to him. He turned and looked at me for just a moment then continued his stare into the woods, with his nostrils quivering as he took in the smells. He now had the look of a predator; he seemed to study all things around him with a calculating interest. I didn't attempt to touch him but wondered what he was seeing and thinking. I hugged my knees then, finally, got up and headed back to bed. I fell back into a fitful sleep, dreading the next morning.

After breakfast, I found the card that Jeff, the ranger from the wild animal farm, had left me and I slowly dialed his number. He lived in a house with his wife at the farm. I hoped he would not be there but, on the second ring, he answered. I identified myself and Jeff said, "Hi, Dawn. What can I do for you?"

"Jeff, I need to come out and see you. We had a little incident here with Parthur, yesterday." I quickly went on to tell him about Parthur's personality changes over the last month and, finally, I told him about the bite. "But I know he didn't mean it." I paused for a few moments. "I guess what I need to know are you still interested in having him at your wild animal farm?

"Absolutely, Dawn. I know how unhappy this makes you but I am glad there were no serious injuries. We would love to have your bobcat here at the farm. Could you come by tomorrow morning, early? Say about 8 o'clock? We don't open until 10 o'clock. That way, I can show you around before the crowds get here and we can talk."

I agreed, sadly.

We talked a little longer and Jeff gave me directions to the ranger house. "Dawn, I know this is hard for you. I do understand."

I hung up the phone. My Dad was standing behind me, as I stood pondering my decision. "You know this is hard for all of us, Dawn," he said.

I had a lump in my throat and couldn't answer him. My eyes were swimming with tears. He patted me on my shoulder, as I moved away into the other room.

Parthur stayed very much to himself the rest of that day at Hawthorn Hill. I would try to find him periodically and, when I did, I decided it was prudent to not bother him. I would have loved to have held him and brushed him as in days gone by but I knew that was not what he wanted.

After another restless night, I dove early the next morning to the wild animal farm and arrived a few minutes before eight. The thirty-mile trip took me about forty-five minutes. Jeff saw me arrive in his driveway as he stood at his kitchen window drinking a cup of coffee. He was out his front door to greet me before I climbed out of my car. Jeff ushered me into the kitchen of the Ranger house and introduced me to his wife, Barbara, who poured me a large mug of steaming black coffee. We sat down at a round kitchen table in front of a large picture window that had a perfect view of much of the wild animal farm. He sat down opposite me. "So, tell me about your bobcat, Dawn. How has he changed?"

I sat stiffly at the ranger's kitchen table while Barbara busied herself at the kitchen sink; I explained Parthur's personality changes, the torn-up teddy bear and how he had snapped at me. "I don't want any of us hurt," I said, "but I feel so responsible for him. How can I place him behind bars for the rest of his life?"

"I know this is a difficult decision for you but you have to believe we will take excellent care of him here. I can hardly wait for you to see his living quarters. We really like to give our felines ample room and, Dawn, we will try to find him a mate," Jeff said. He went on about the philosophy of the wild animal farm and their interests in the wellbeing of each animal.

I sat in silence, listening and thinking about all that he had said.

"Let me show you where he will live. Maybe that would make you feel better."

We left the ranger's house and proceeded down a manicured path that led straight into the middle of several large structures. I was impressed with the tidy appearance of the grounds and the well-maintained buildings. We entered a big, barn-like structure lined on one wall with four large cages. The first cage contained a big male lion with a huge tawny mane. He was sound asleep on a ledge in the back of his cage. Several large balls littered his cage floor. Next to his cage was a female lion. She was pacing back and forth in front of her bars. I stopped for a minute in front of her cage to look into her eyes. The lioness ignored me.

Jeff ushered me to the next cage and indicated this would be Parthur's home. It was empty except for a large, bare tree trunk that went from the floor to the ceiling and had several limbs spreading out three feet from the main trunk. The sun was streaming in from an over-head sky light. It was a nice area, to be sure, but it was the bars that almost brought me to tears.

Jeff sensed what I was feeling and said, "We will do everything we can to make Parthur as happy as possible here." He pointed to the back of the cage where there was a large door. "That door in the back leads out to a large outdoor area with trees, rocks and lots of space for him to play. He will be able to get lots of exercise." He paused for a minute, "You can come and see him as often as you like."

Deep down, I knew there really weren't many alternatives. I had a good feeling about Jeff Long. He was a kind man who loved working with animals and I knew he would do his best for my bobcat but I wished I could keep Parthur. I looked back into the empty cage. This wasn't how I wanted to see my pet for the rest of his life but what could I do?

I stood in front of the cage for some time. Jeff moved away from me to give me space to think. He had stepped over to the female lion's cage. The young lioness had stopped her pacing and Jeff was reaching through the bars to scratch her around her neck. She stretched and leaned up against the bars as he hit the real itchy spots. I liked what I saw.

"All right," I said. "I'll bring him over tomorrow," I hesitated for just a minute, "but you have to promise me one thing."

"What's that?" asked Jeff.

"You must promise me that you will find him a mate."

Jeff walked over to me and took my hand. "You have my word on that. We would love to raise little bobcats here."

I left the wild animal farm as fast as I could. I was miserable all the way home. I felt as if I had betrayed a good friend. *How could I do this to a pet I loved? But what other options did I have?* The questions repeated themselves over and over in my mind, with no answers. When I got to my parents' home, I looked for Parthur as I entered the back door. It used to be that when he heard the back-door slam, he would rush into the kitchen to see who had arrived but there was no Parthur. I was certain he was probably under some bed in the house.

My mom, dad and I spent a quiet evening together that night, each of us deep in our own thoughts. Parthur made a couple of appearances but he moved away from each of us when we tried to touch him. My dad saw the hurt in my eyes as Parthur rebuffed me. No one slept well that night, especially me. I got up in the middle of the night again, looking for Parthur. He was on the big porch but this time he was looking out toward the river with his nose turned into the soft breeze coming from that direction.

Parthur was again remembering the night he had spent outside, wandering around Hawthorn Hill, the moon-light dance in the small meadow and his encounter with the tiny mouse. He couldn't have known bobcats have a biological need to hunt, chase and capture lively moving objects and the excitement of the hunt nourishes a bobcat's nervous system* but he did know there was something out there pulling at him. He loved Dawn but there was such a strong longing for all the wonders lying outside that screened-in porch.

I sat next to him for a while and watched his nose quiver as he smelled the smells of the night. I didn't touch him. After a while, I softly got up and returned to bed. I tossed and turned for the rest of the night. Finally, it was morning.

Parthur

Chapter 22

I had told Jeff I would bring Parthur and meet him at the ranger house around 8 o'clock, just as I had the day before. Because it would take almost an hour to get there, I needed to leave at 7 o'clocki. I watched Parthur eat his breakfast. It was just a few minutes past 7 o'clock when I picked him up to take him to my car.

I hadn't carried him in a while and I was surprised at his weight. He really was a beautiful specimen of an adult bobcat now. As usual, he hung limp in my arms. As I reached the screened door, my dad and mom stopped me and each patted a 'goodbye' on Parthur's head. No one said anything. No one could speak. I was out the door and down the back steps with my heavy bundle. I placed Parthur in the passenger's seat of my car, closed the door and headed to the driver's side. As I was getting into my car, I looked back to the small back porch where my parents were standing. My dad had his arm around my mom's shoulders and my mom was wiping her eyes with the edge of her apron. My eyes filled with tears, once again, as I sat down in the driver's seat of my car. I quickly wiped my eyes with the back of my hand, started the engine of the little car and backed around so I was headed down the gravel driveway. I made my way down the bumpy road to the highway.

Parthur was very quiet all the way to the wild animal farm. He sat sedately in the front passenger seat the whole way there. He sensed something major was about to happen and he chose to just sit and wait. Never once did he jump up to his usual place behind my head on the back of the driver's seat. I kept looking for signs of the old Parthur because this new Parthur was so foreign to me. I kept looking over at him, perplexed with his mood and aloof demeanor. "Parthur, please don't hate me," I whispered.

Jeff Long was standing outside his front door as I drove up. He had a large carrying cage at his side. He picked it up and moved toward my car.

"That won't be necessary," I said. "I will carry him."

"Isn't he a little heavy?" Jeff asked.

"I don't mind," I answered. I knew he didn't like the idea I would be carrying Parthur to his new home but I didn't care. This was my last time to hold him. I wasn't going to give that up. I got out of the car and leaned back in and picked up Parthur. With a little bit of effort, I finally got him adjusted and comfortable in my arms. Jeff closed my car door and the two of us walked in silence toward the big-cat barn.

Jeff kept looking over at me and Parthur. He was worried the cat was too heavy for me and he also worried the cat would jump out of my arms. Parthur never moved. His inquisitive eyes were taking in everything, however, and he loved all the new animal smells.

When we reached the big-cat house, Jeff opened the door for Parthur and me. We walked in front of the big male lion then the female. Parthur's nose quivered with their scents. I felt him stiffen a little in my arms. Then we were in front of Parthur's new home with the big bare tree. There were all sorts of balls and toys strewn around the floor and a small ledge had been placed on the rear wall of the cage. The front door to the cage was open. I climbed the three steps in front of the door and walked into Parthur's new home, clutching him to my chest.

Jeff stood back as I buried my face into Parthur's soft fur. I dropped down on my knees. "You know I love you," I whispered. "Please don't hate me for this." My tears were matting his fur, and he wiggled with impatience for me to release my grasp now that we were at floor level. Finally, I sighed and placed the bobcat on the floor of the cage and let go. He bounded away from me, scurried up the tree trunk and took a position in the crotch of the largest branch. He sat down and began to clean himself, ignoring Jeff and me. I backed out of the cage, and Jeff secured the door. I stood there for some time, looking in through the bars then I left.

The trip back to Hawthorn Hill was a sad one. I felt empty and drained. I had so many doubts and questions. How would Parthur handle this new lifestyle, would he be happy there and would he miss me? I knew I would desperately miss him. I wondered what Parthur would think of all those people who would come and stare at him. I was so in hopes Jeff would be able to find him a mate. The tears never stopped rolling down my face. At one point I was crying so hard I had to pull over to the side of the road to get control of myself but I finally made it home.

When I got back to Hawthorn Hill, my mom was busy baking some cookies in the kitchen. Our eyes met as I entered the kitchen and I could see my mom had been crying, too. We hugged. "Oh, Mom, I hope I've done the right thing."

Parthur

Chapter 23

I had to leave Illinois for Yuma in only three weeks for my teaching job and the new fall year at Kofa High School. I didn't want Parthur to think I had forsaken him so I tried to make a visit to the animal farm every other day. Jeff suggested I always arrive at the farm before visiting hours. That way, my visits could be more private. I was usually there by 8 o'clock in the morning. As the days wore on, Parthur became more and more distant each time I arrived.

I would stand outside the bars of the cage and call to him, "Parthur, Parthur, it's me." On the first few visits he trotted right up to me and I would scratch him through the bars and stroke and pet him but, as the days rolled by, he began to ignore me. One week before I was to return to Yuma, he even growled at me, as I stood outside the cage. I was heartbroken. He seemed to have changed so completely. He was as a wild animal now and I hardly recognized him. I felt helpless to change the situation.

I didn't stop visiting Parthur for that last week, even though he would have nothing to do with me. The days were rushing by and soon I would have to leave for Arizona. The morning before I was to start my trip west, I once again stood in front of Parthur's cage. I whispered my goodbyes to the bobcat, as he sat on the ledge in the back of the cage, ignoring me. "I'm sorry I had to do this to you, Parthur. Please forgive me." He turned his head and looked at me with an unblinking stare. His only movement was the occasional twitch of his little tail.

Then I had an idea. I reached my arm in through the bars and gave him the "thumbs up" sign. I stood there for several moments with my arm outstretched with the 'thumbs up' sign and waited. Parthur stared hard at me. He lifted one front paw and then set it down again. He then turned and looked away. I was devastated by the rebuff but I stayed in front of his cage for almost an hour that morning. He never looked my way again and, finally, I left.

When I got home, my dad was sitting at the kitchen table. "Dad, will you please go visit Parthur after I leave? I don't want him to think we have given up on him."

"Sure. I'll stop by and see him," my dad answered. "Was there any change in his attitude toward you today?"

"No," I answered in a low voice. "Dad, do you think I did the right thing?"

"I don't know, Dawn. We could not have kept him here. I am certain of that. That's the trouble with trying to make a pet out of a wild animal. They are meant to be free."

"I just wish there had been something else I could have done."

"I know," my dad answered. "I'll keep track of him for you after you leave. You can be certain of that."

With a heavy heart I started my trip back to Yuma the next day. My car seemed so empty. I remembered our last drive to the wild animal farm. He had changed so much. Now I was all alone in my little car as I headed west on the interstate.

Two days later, I passed through Gila Bend, Arizona. I thought about Nancy and Jack Copeland, and the night I had received the baby bobcat from them. From the highway I could see the truck stop where Nancy worked. I could not bring myself to stop. I felt guilty and I felt as if I had let everyone down, especially Parthur. I had failed. I did think back to the memories of that October night so many months ago and the four girls from my "golf team", who had shared the beginning of it all with me. This wasn't the way I had wanted it to turn out. With all those troubling thoughts, I made it back to Yuma.

Parthur

Chapter 24

Berle, had stayed in Yuma for the summer. She still had our apartment and was glad to have me back. Her little dog, Twitch, even seemed happy to see me again. When I entered the apartment, the little dog ran to my feet, begging to be held. I lifted him to my face and he rewarded me with a big lick across my check. It made me laugh.

I had talked to Berle on the phone several times over the summer so she knew some of the details concerning Parthur. "What is the latest on Parthur?"

"It's not good," I answered. "The morning before I left the Quad Cities, I stopped off at the wild animal farm to see him just one more time. I was so hoping his demeanor there would have changed," I paused for just a moment as I thought about that last visit. "He just ignored me and wouldn't even look my way. It really broke my heart. Gosh, Berle, I feel so guilty about him. I don't know how I thought this was all going to turn out but certainly not like this. Surely there must have been something I could have done."

"I know you did your best, Dawn. You shouldn't be so hard on yourself."

"My dad is going to keep tabs on him for me."

"Maybe there will be a change," Berle offered.

I didn't think so and I quickly changed the subject because it was too painful to think about Parthur in a cage. "Hey, how was your summer here? What's new here at the apartments?"

Berle filled me in. Most of the teachers Berle and I hung around with were already back. A big group of them were going to meet for Chinese food and a movie that night. That sounded great to me.

When I got home that evening, I felt a little guilty I hadn't thought about Parthur back in Illinois all evening. Berle evidently had cautioned all our friends not to bring up the topic so no one had asked about Parthur. As I crawled into bed that night, the questions rolled over and over again in my mind. *Did I use Parthur as just a novelty then throw him away when the times got difficult? Was I selfish in trying to keep him as my pet? My dad warned me about trying to make a pet out of a wild animal. Was it possible? Maybe I gave up too quickly and missed something.*

Parthur

Surely there was something I could have done differently. I tossed and turned but finally fell asleep.

My second year of teaching at Kofa High School had many demands on my time. I was still the yearbook advisor and I also had volunteered to direct the school's fall play. Life was busy and full. I loved my students and my job.

In one of the many conversations on the phone I had with my dad about Parthur, I asked, "Dad, what about a mate for him? What does Jeff say?"

"I saw Jeff just a week ago. He said they were working on it," my dad replied yet there still had been no change in Parthur's demeanor. He was just as distant to my dad as he had been to me. I had hoped, with time, there would have been a flicker of response to my dad on his visits but I was not surprised when there wasn't.

Parthur

Chapter 25

In late October, I received a phone call from my dad that broke my heart. "Dawn, I've got some bad news for you," he began then he hesitated.

"Dad, what is it?" I sensed from the tone of my father's voice something terrible had happened. I clutched the phone to my head in fear of what he would say next.

"It's about Parthur," he continued.

Some of the dread left me. *At least the bad news isn't about a family member but what is the bad news about Parthur?* "Oh, Dad, what has happened?" I whispered.

There was a long pause as my dad composed himself. "Jeff Long, the ranger from the wild animal farm, just called me a few minutes ago." There was another long pause and I held my breath, fearing what my dad was going to say next. "Dawn, he told me Parthur died."

"Oh, no," I wailed. Tears flooded my eyes. I had been standing and I now slumped down into a chair next to the phone. Neither my father nor I could speak for a few minutes but finally, I choked out, "How did it happened?"

Berle had been in the kitchen when she heard that painful cry from me. She rushed over to my side, knelt down and mouthed noiselessly, "What happened?"

My face was ashen and tears were slipping down my cheeks. I silently mouthed the words, "Parthur is dead." Berle was stunned. She knew what this meant to me. She leaned over and gave me a hug and then patted my hand. She quietly moved away from me so I could talk to my dad.

His voice was ragged but he related what few details he had, "Seems Parthur got sick." There was another long pause. "Jeff said he just didn't recover."

Again, there was a long silence as the two of us struggled with this news and our emotions. "Dad, maybe it is for the best," I whispered through my tears. "I don't think he ever liked it there."

My dad agreed.

Neither of us said much more as we ended our telephone conversation. I slowly replaced the phone receiver and was consumed with my loss. I felt so responsible for what had happened. What more could I have done to have saved Parthur and prevented this outcome? "Oh, Parthur," I whispered. "I am so sorry." Then I put my face in my hands and cried deep painful sobs.

Parthur

Chapter 26

With the loss of Parthur, one of the hardest things for me to do was to tell my students at Kofa High the sad ending of his story, especially my "golf team". They were as devastated as I was about his death, since they had all been with me the night I brought him home from Gila Bend. Amy Stanton took it the hardest when she heard the sad news. Oh, Miss Fritz, I am so sorry," and she threw her arms around me and sobbed.

I tried to comfort her as best I could but the pain of the loss was too new for me, as well. I put my arms around the girl's shoulders and we both cried softly together. I than pulled away from her and held her by her shoulders, "It's probably for the best,

Amy. I don't think he liked it there in that cage. I know I didn't like it he was there."

As the days passed, the ache of Parthur's death became less sharp. I threw myself into my teaching duties. The fall play I was directing was deep into after school practice and the yearbook staff was hard at work on layouts and photos for that year's book. So, time flew and I had little time to dwell on my loss and sadness, as well as my guilt. I was glad of that.

The Saturday before Thanksgiving weekend I got a call from the editor of Kofa High's yearbook. "Hello, Miss Fritz?"

"Yes," I answered.

"This is Tom Sommers"

"Yes, Tom. What can I do for you?"

"Well, there is a group of us from the yearbook staff who would like to come by and see you. Would that be all right?"

"Sure, Tom," I replied hesitantly. "Is there something wrong?" I was somewhat confused by his request. I didn't normally have visits from my students at my apartment but I was the yearbook advisor and I certainly was not going to turn them away. It was an unusual request but Tom sounded as if he had something important he wanted to discuss with me.

"No, no. There's nothing wrong," he insisted. "We could be there in fifteen minutes. Would that be all right?"

"Well, I guess, Tom. Do you know where I live?"

"The Fairway Apartments, right?"

"That's right. Apartment Number 3."

Parthur

"Great. We'll be there in just a few minutes." He hung up, hurriedly.

I waited for my students to arrive, wondering what on earth was so important they had to come and see me on a Saturday. Berle had left early that morning and had taken Twitch with her so I was home alone in the apartment.

Suddenly, there was a knock at the apartment door. When I opened the door, standing there were five of the La Corona Yearbook staff members with big grins on their faces. Tom Sommers stepped forward. "Miss Fritz, we know how badly you felt when Parthur died." He hesitated for just a moment, and then someone punched him to go on. "Well, we decided you needed a new pet. This is what we found for you."

With that, Amy Stanton stepped from behind Tom. In her arms was a fluffy, coal-black kitten. "Miss Harper, we know we could never replace Parthur but maybe you would enjoy this kitten." She held it out toward me. "His name is Mully, for Mulligan. You know, golfers take another shot when they don't like their first shot and call it a Mulligan." She hesitated for just a second. "I didn't mean you didn't like Parthur," she stammered. Her face flushed red.

I was stunned.

"He's six-weeks-old and he's ready for a new home," Amy continued. She looked carefully at me. "Would you like him?"

"I don't know what to say," I stammered.

"Just say you want him," Tom said, with a nervous laugh.

"I would be honored to have him." I reached out to take the fluffy baby kitten from Amy and cradled him in my arms. The little, bright-eyed kitten looked up into my face and then licked my fingers. *Just like Parthur*, I thought.

"See, he likes you," Amy said.

"He is absolutely darling. Where did he come from?"

"Well, our cat had kittens again," said Amy. "This was the cutest one."

"Amy, he is adorable. I love him." I had tears in my eyes as I looked into the young, eager faces in front of me. "I don't know what to say. I can't tell you what this means to me. Thank you very, very much, each of you." My voice broke as I pressed the soft little kitten to my cheek. With that, the kitten licked the side of my face. Everyone laughed.

I invited the five students into the apartment. Each of them had something for the little kitten. There was a plastic litter box, a big bag of kitty litter, several cans of cat food and two small bowls; one for food and one for water. I was absolutely amazed at the thoughtfulness of these youngsters. I was filled with the warmth of their generosity.

"Well, we had better get going," Tom said. "We need to let you get used to Mully."

I thanked the students over and over as they left my apartment. I cradled the small, fluffy kitten in the crook of my arm as they walked out the door. As soon as they had all left, I walked back to the couch and placed the small animal in the middle of a plump pillow. I looked down at him with a smile. "You know, Mully, you can never take the place of Parthur but I think I've got plenty of love left over for you. I do wonder what Twitch is going to think of you, though. You both are small but I do believe he is a little bigger than you." The little dog, Twitch, was a good-natured dog. I was certain there would be no problem.

As if on cue, the black kitten moved its tail back and forth and made small mewing sounds as it looked up at me. I laughed, reached down and scooped up the kitten in my arms and did a little waltz around the living room. "We're going to have lots of fun together."

Chapter 27

The end of October, a month earlier.

In the ranger house at the wild animal farm in Moline, Illinois, Jeff Long hung up the phone with a sigh. His wife, Barbara, looked at him. "Jeff, shouldn't you have just told him the truth?"

"How could I?" Jeff replied angrily. "How could I tell him that I had just let their pet bobcat jump over the wall and escape?"

"But they loved that animal so much," his wife replied, softly.

"I know. I know." Jeff retorted. He thought for just a moment and made a deep sigh. "I'm sorry. I didn't mean to take it out on you. I feel so responsible for what happened. I know how much that animal means to Dawn and her family." He stopped and thought about the situation again and hesitated. "There is no way that cat can make it on its own. I am certain he lacks the hunting capabilities he'll need for survival. I didn't want the Fritz family to think about him in the wild, slowly starving to death. I decided it was just better they thought he was already dead."

Barbara sat quietly at the kitchen table. She and Jeff both loved the wild animal farm. She knew Jeff was probably right but she also knew how devastated the Fritzes would be over the supposed death of their bobcat. She and Jeff had both watched Dawn and Ken visit the animal on so many occasions. "Do you think their bobcat might have a slight chance out on its own?" she asked.

"I don't think so," Jeff replied. "When I told Ken Fritz the cat was dead, I didn't think I was far from wrong," he paused for a moment. "Their cat was raised all its life in their home. He is a full-grown bobcat now, with none of the skills he needs to live in the wild. How could he ever survive one of our Illinois winters?" Jeff was out of his chair now, pacing back and forth in front of the big picture window at the ranger house. He stopped and looked out the window. He was angry with himself as he thought back over the cat's escape. How could he have let this happen?

It had all started eight days ago. The Fritz's bobcat had stopped eating for some reason or another. Jeff had tried everything he could think of. He even brought in pieces of chicken to tempt the bobcat's appetite. Dawn had told him that was his favorite meal. It was to no avail. He just could not coax the young cat to take any nourishment. Jeff called the vet. He also could not find a reason why the young animal would not eat. He had taken blood and urine samples but all the tests were negative to any of the diseases the vet could think of. The animal was taking water. That was the only good sign.

On the fourth day of the cat's fast, Parthur had become lethargic. Jeff stood outside his cage and watched him with great concern. "What's the problem, Parthur? I wish you could tell me," he whispered to the listless animal.

On the fifth morning, Jeff opened Parthur's cage and carefully picked up the sick animal. He put him in a carrying cage and transported him quickly up the path to the ranger house. As Jeff entered the kitchen, Barbara saw the concern in his eyes. He had told her earlier that morning at breakfast he planned to try and nurse the animal back to health at the ranger house. She had already made a makeshift bed for the cat out of a large wooden box and old terry towels. "I hate to do this to you, Barbara," Jeff said as he gently pulled the sick animal out of the carrying cage and placed him in the box she had fixed. "I don't know what else to do. He was a house pet for almost a year. Maybe if we keep him in here with us, I can snap him out of it."

The cat opened his eyes as Jeff moved him but they were now shut as he lay in the make-shift bed.

"It's all right. I understand." Over the years Barbara had become used to sharing her home with strange creatures. This wasn't the first time Jeff had brought an ailing animal home.

Parthur

Parthur lay lethargically in the box in the Long's' kitchen for another day. Jeff was able to get some liquids into the animal and a small amount of food.

The following day, Parthur looked a little better. He responded to the pats and strokes from the ranger and his wife. Jeff convinced the cat to eat some solid food. Parthur slowly nibbled at it as Jeff watched. Jeff smiled and patted the cat on his head. "I think you are going to make it now," he said. Parthur had finally turned the corner and Jeff was certain the cat was on the mend. Jeff had spent much of his time for the last two days nursing the bobcat. He was pleased his hard work and concern had paid off.

"We'll keep him here in our house for just one more day," he told his wife. "I'll move him back out to his cage tomorrow morning. Is that all right with you, Barb?"

Barbara nodded. She had enjoyed having the beautiful animal in her kitchen. She had spent as much time as she could, petting and stroking his body while he was so sick. Now, he lifted his head and looked at her. She reached over and gave him another pat. Parthur closed his eyes in appreciation and pushed against her hand.

Parthur wasn't sure why he had gotten so sick but he could feel his body was on the mend. He had felt hot and listless before but that was all behind him now. He curled up into a ball and took a long peaceful nap among the old terry towels that made up his bed. He felt his strength returning.

When Jeff and Barbara went to bed that night, they closed the door to the kitchen area but left out some food for the sick animal, just in case his appetite got better. Parthur smelled the tempting meal. Soon after the Longs were asleep, he rose from his sickbed and devoured every bit of it. He licked his face and paws and then took a long drink at the water bowl they had left next to the food. He also used the sand box that was placed nearby.

By morning, he was feeling fit. He was up early and explored the kitchen where he had been left. He jumped up on the kitchen table and smelled the apples that were in a large bowl in the center of the table. He liked their smell. Then he hopped down, looked around and then jumped up on the kitchen counter. Barbara had a cookie jar that was half filled with cookies. He could smell their sweet smell but the top was quite secure. He couldn't get at them. He pawed at the jar and it moved a bit. He pawed at it again. The jar was just about ready to topple off the counter when Jeff and Barbara opened the kitchen door.

"Well," Jeff said, "look who's feeling pretty feisty this morning." The young bobcat jumped off the counter and jumped up on one of the kitchen chairs and eyed him.

Barbara pushed the cookie jar back in its place.

"I'll take him out to his cage right after breakfast," he said to Barbara. Jeff went to the refrigerator and found two large pieces of chicken.

Parthur watched as he placed the raw meat in his dish. Without much hesitation, the hungry animal jumped down from the chair and quickly devoured both pieces.

Parthur

"Looks like you've got your appetite back for sure," Jeff said with a sigh of relief as he knelt, watching Parthur.

Barbara started to fix breakfast but she kept one eye on the cat. She really wasn't afraid of him but she had a healthy respect for wild animals. "Jeff, when you're finished there, would you please take out the garbage, before you go out to the cat barn?" she asked, over her shoulder.

"Sure," said Jeff as he stood up. He walked over to the mud room that also had a door that led out to the back yard. Barbara had neatly piled four large, black plastic sacks right by the back door. All four bags were filled to capacity and were bulging with their contents. "Why is there so much?"

"We missed garbage day last week."

Jeff wrapped his arms around two of the bundles then used his two hands to awkwardly carry the other two bags. He was just able to get the back door open with two fingers on his right hand. He shoved his foot into the small opening to pull the door further open, so he could get through it with his ungainly load.

Suddenly, Parthur sprang. He shot through Jeff's feet and bolted out the door. Jeff dropped the garbage bags and they burst open showering the floor with coffee grounds, vegetable and fruit remnants, tin cans and all sorts of sticky and gooey materials. In Jeff's rush to chase after the fleeing animal, his feet went out from under him and he fell into the garbage pile at the doorway. After much slipping and sliding, he finally got back on his feet and was out the door in hot pursuit.

The Longs' back yard had a six-foot concrete wall around it with a side gate. It had been built so Jeff could use it while he worked with some of the animals. Jeff quickly checked to see if the side gate was secure and it was. Jeff knew, though, the wall was no match for the jumping capabilities of the young cat. Parthur was standing at the far end of the yard and he turned and faced Jeff. His short tail was twitching excitedly back and forth. The cat stood very still and alert. He watched as Jeff slowly approached him.

Jeff held his hands out in front of him in a pleading gesture to the watching animal. "Here, Parthur," Jeff called. "Come to me, please," he softly called. For a minute, as he stepped closer to the animal, Jeff thought the cat would stand still and he could grab him. At the last second, however, Parthur jumped away.

At first, it was just a game to Parthur, a game Jeff was not going to win unless Parthur chose to let him win. The cat was just too fast and too agile. Then something deep inside Parthur's brain clicked and his instincts took over. He lifted his head and sniffed the air, sniffed it again then, with one graceful move, he hopped effortlessly up on top of the six-foot wall that surrounded the back yard. Parthur hesitated for just one more second. He turned and took one last look at the ranger as Jeff frantically made a lunge to capture him. The cat glanced into the thicket on the other side of the wall, crouched and jumped into the low tangled brush below the trees. He was gone.

Jeff looked mournfully over the wall. There was no sign of the fleeing bobcat.

Chapter 28

After Parthur scaled the wall around the ranger house's patio, he never looked back. Something deep inside his brain told him to head northeast. He didn't know why he was heading in that direction but he trotted off as quickly as he could in the underbrush in a northeasterly direction, testing the air periodically as he went along. The thicket into which he had disappeared around the ranger's house lasted for only half a mile. The brush became less and less dense as he continued and Parthur sensed he was getting close to humans and houses.

Suddenly, he broke through the last of the thicket and was looking down on a new subdivision of small homes. He sat down in the cover of a small bush and considered what to do next. He was still a little thin from his sickness but the two hearty meals he had consumed before he left the ranger's house had helped considerably. All his life humans had provided him with his meals. Now, his stomach was growling and he was going to have to find something on his own.

Parthur stayed close to the edge of the thicket for several hours. A soft wind blew from his right and made the bush he was hiding under sway to the rhythm of the breeze but by midday it had shifted. Now the breeze was coming from the direction of the houses. In that breeze, he detected the faint odor of chicken. His nose quivered and a little drool formed at his lips. Parthur left the security of the underbrush and headed straight for the smell.

What Parthur smelled came from a nearby garbage can that sat behind a small garage attached to one of the houses that stood on the edge of the development. It was garbage pick-up day for the local residents. The lid to the garbage can that offered up the tantalizing aroma was a little askew and the distinctive carton of Kentucky Fried Chicken was just visible. Parthur approached the can tentatively. He walked around and around it and then stood on his hind legs to see inside. He easily knocked the lid off the tin garbage can; it hit the blacktop with a terrible clatter. Undaunted by the noise, Parthur jumped and was on top of the exposed garbage, and within seconds his head was completely buried in the round, red and white container. In it he found three pieces of chicken; a feast.

While Parthur was devouring one of the pieces of chicken, a large golden retriever dog came around the corner of the garage. He had heard the garbage can lid hit the street and had come to investigate the noise. When he saw the large cat in his family's garbage can, he stopped and barked a warning. That always scared the cats away and he hated cats. But this cat didn't move and he seemed quite large. He moved a little closer and barked again. Parthur lifted his head out of the cardboard container and looked at the dog. He remembered Ken Harper's dogs at Hawthorn Hill. He remembered how he had intimidated them from inside the screens on the large wrap-around porch. He didn't have any screens here, though.

The large yellow dog was beside himself at the audacity of this large feline and he decided to charge this arrogant cat that was on his family's garbage can. As the dog rushed at the cat with a growl, Parthur decided to hold his position on top of the garbage can. He snarled a long, low rumbling, growl himself and gave an angry hiss curled back his lips and showed his fangs.

The agitated yellow dog halted just in front of the garbage can and made a snapping lunge at the large cat. Parthur lifted one of his front paws and slapped at the dog's face with his razor-sharp claws. He connected with the retriever's nose. The dog yipped with pain as blood spurted from the wound. The dog was stunned. Never had he faced a cat that had stood up to him and never had he encountered one that had hurt him. They always ran away. The angry dog hesitated and considered if he should make another cautious advance at this aggressive cat, while barking his distaste of his presence. That was all the time Parthur needed. He grabbed two of the three pieces of chicken out of the bucket, was off the garbage can in a flash and on his way back to the cover of the thicket.

The golden retriever gave chase only halfheartedly. His nose was bleeding quite badly now, and it really hurt. He stopped his chase at the edge of the thicket where he had seen the cat disappear. He stood there and barked a, "You had better not return," warning several times. He decided not to follow but he stood there for over fifteen minutes warning the cat not to come back. His nose dripped bright red blood into the grass.

Parthur calmly bounded through the underbrush and into a small wood. He quickly put quite a bit of distant between himself and that pesky dog. Finally, he stopped and listened. His ears quivered as he listened for the animal's barks. They were faint and far away. Parthur started out again in a northeasterly direction at a slow trot, giving the housing subdivision and the dog a wide berth. He still had the two pieces of chicken in his mouth and when he found a nice secluded spot, he stopped and finished them.

He rested for a while once he had finished his meal. He thought about his encounter with that big yellow dog. He decided it was probably a good idea to stay away from all dogs. He licked up the few scraps of chicken that had fallen into the grass in front of him, cleaned his face and paws and started out again.

The trees and underbrush that had hidden the cat were beginning to thin again. Parthur could hear the sounds of traffic in front of him with the low hum of many tires over pavement. He came out on top of a small hill and looked down on a major highway that had four lanes of traffic rushing back and forth; two heading north and two heading south. He sat down in the tall yellow and brown grass and watched the cars and trucks speeding back and forth only fifty feet from where he lay. His head went left then right then left again, as he watched the vehicles with interest as they swept past him. If anyone in any of those cars had looked over in his direction, they probably would not have seen him. Only Parthur's head was visible above the tall grass, and his tawny fur blended in with the dead stalks that surrounded him. Parthur didn't really feel threatened by the cars. He had ridden dozens of times in Dawn's car and had loved it but this was different. He wasn't in one of these cars but was watching them. He felt compelled to cross this road but something told him there was danger here. He would have to be very careful.

The young cat crept away from the tall grass area and backed into the cover of a small thicket and waited. He took several short naps, walked back out to look at the traffic twice but then went back and waited some more, in the secluded bushes of the thicket.

A soft pink and blue twilight arrived then it was night. Once more, he moved out of the protection of the thicket and sat in the tall grass near the road. The northeasterly path he was following led straight across this road. He must get to the other side.

Finally, he decided it was time to make his move. The muscles in his body tensed as he tried to choose the best moment to make the dash to the other side. In the dark, the cars and trucks didn't look as big and dangerous. The noise was still there but now it was only moving lights. He raised his powerful haunches just slightly in preparation for his charge. There was a short lull in traffic and suddenly he made his dash. He made it across the first two lanes without a problem. He was now in the narrow, grassy median. He didn't slow his forward motion, even though there was a lone car heading north that was bearing down on him. The adrenaline was pumping in his veins as he pushed his body with a furious effort to make it across.

The northbound driver saw the blur of yellow fur race in front of his head lights. He slammed on his brakes and his tires squealed as they slid on the concrete. He missed the animal only by inches. Fortunately, there had been no other cars around him.

"What was that?" the driver asked his wife, incredulously.

"I don't know. It looked like some kind of large cat." she answered. As their car picked up speed and continued up the road, they both turned around for a second to look out the rear window. It was dark, and Parthur was long gone.

"It looked like a bobcat but what would a bobcat be doing in the city?" the driver asked. He shook his head in wonder and continued his drive north along the highway. The driver and his wife were shaken by the near miss.

The incident had frightened Parthur, as well. His heart was pounding wildly. He ran for almost a mile without stopping. He passed by houses, a park then he was back into a wooded area. He always kept to his northeasterly direction, however. Parthur decided cars could be dangerous even though he had ridden in them so many times with Dawn. He would try to avoid them as much as he could, as he headed in his chosen direction.

Chapter 29

In the next few weeks, as Parthur moved in his northeasterly direction, he had several other close encounters with dogs. Most of them were little animals, which he didn't fear at all but he hated their insistent, high pitched barking. Parthur was a quiet animal and the noise they created was an irritant to his ears. He kept his distance from most of them but a couple of times Parthur had been surprised by big dogs. Fortunately, Parthur was quite quick and he eluded their clumsy chases. In reality, if Parthur had been forced into a fight with one of the larger canines, Parthur would have been the winner. A dog really does not have much of a chance in a head-on conflict with a bobcat and Parthur was a big bobcat.

It seemed to him, he'd run into more dogs in the areas where there were houses. So now, Parthur was trying to stay clear of neighborhoods but the northeasterly heading he was following led him straight through some heavily populated areas. He frightened more than one human as he made his mad dashes between houses on his way from one area to another.

Because of the terrain, roads and population, Parthur was now heading straight east. It wasn't long before he encountered the Rock River. It was a narrow, fast-moving stream that had sporadic houses along its shores. Because it was Fall, several of these houses stood empty, their owners only there in the summertime. Parthur liked all the trees and underbrush along the fast-paced river so he followed its shore east for several miles.

There had been many days when Parthur couldn't find any food and his stomach would grumble with emptiness. He had scavenged a couple more garbage cans but some of the food he had found was rancid. Garbage cans also meant more dogs and he wanted to avoid them if possible. He had stumbled across some roadkill on some of the roads he crossed, and that filled his belly for a while. When he discovered rabbits, however, his food problems were solved.

Imprinted in his memory was a predator-prey association that extended back in time, perhaps two million years*. The urge to stalk and kill rabbits was primordial and compulsive. His first kill was almost by accident. He had curled up under a bush in a bed of yellow-gray grass with an empty stomach for an afternoon nap. He was awakened by the soft munching sounds of a large gray cottontail that had hopped within five feet of where Parthur was half hidden. The rabbit, not knowing that danger was nearby, hopped a few more inches closer to the attentive cat, while it grazed on some sprigs of green grass that had pushed their way in among the dead grasses. Parthur discovered he enjoyed keeping his presence a secret from the creature he was watching and he stayed motionless, eying carefully the animal's every movement. The rabbit moved even closer as it ate its dinner. Parthur could see the rapid chewing motion of the rabbit's jaw as it now calmly nibbled at some weeds, unaware that the young cat was so near.

Instinctively, Parthur knew what to do. He carefully flattened himself to the ground and, with his hind feet; he ever so slightly began to knead the earth in eager anticipation of his lunge. He pounced on the rabbit and killed it quickly, with an instinctive snap and a quick bite at the nape of its neck. He growled and chattered as he tore into the rabbit's hide. It had been a long time since his last meal and he was giving warning to any animal within earshot he was not going to share this prize. He decided he liked rabbit almost as much as chicken.

Parthur later discovered frogs and toads. Frogs tasted great but he soon understood he had to be quite fast and quiet to have a chance of getting one without getting wet. On the banks of the Rock River, he learned to creep with his belly low to the ground and his elbows bowed as his paws crept soundlessly over every pebble and stick as he stalked these small green and gray animals that called this river home.

Many times, they were just too fast for him and he ended up with a face full of mud and water.

Toads were different, however. Parthur had come upon a big fat one dozing in the grass next to a path the cat had been using near the Rock River. It hadn't even tried to get away from him when he pushed it with one of his front paws. Parthur quickly picked it up in his mouth to take it to a shaded area to have a snack. Almost immediately, the toad let off a watery secretion that tasted terrible. Parthur dropped the toad and shook his head and tongue trying rid himself of the terrible taste. The toad just sat where Parthur had dropped him. Parthur eyed the bumpy, squat animal and walked around and around him as he continued to shake his head. Saliva sprayed out of his mouth as he shook his head harder and harder to try to rid himself of that awful secretion. Surely this animal was good to eat, he thought. Once more, he picked up the toad in his mouth and immediately the toad hit him again with his special excretion. Parthur quickly dropped the toad again, abandoning any idea of eating him and went straight to the river to cleanse his mouth.

Mice were great fun to catch. Parthur remembered that night at Hawthorn Hill when he had encountered one of these tiny creatures. He now had learned to stalk them in the large fields that ran up against the river. It was a game of patience. Parthur used his eyes and ears to locate this small prey, never his sense of smell. He could hear a rustle or a squeak a hundred yards away*. Then he would creep to within pouncing distance without detection. In mastering the hunt, he learned to lie in wait for long periods of time, with the expectation that small movements from his prey would give him their location so he could quietly move into position. He had the heart and courage of a predator and, with each kill, he was getting the experience he would need to survive. Between the mice and the rabbits, he was rarely hungry now.

One afternoon, he came across a mole as it was blindly making its way from one hole to another. It looked like a mouse, only bigger and with no tail but when Parthur grabbed it in his mouth, it tasted terrible. The young cat dropped it, and the mole remained motionless. Parthur sat down on his haunches and started to play with it by knocking it back and forth with his paws. The mole never tried to get away but each time Parthur picked it up in his mouth, it left an awful taste on his tongue and made him drool. He shook his head several times, trying to rid his mouth of the taste. He didn't kill the animal but he did play with it for some time. Finally, Parthur decided to just let it go. When it didn't move right away, he gave it a push with his paw. Finally, the mole moved slowly away from the cat. Parthur watched it go.

Then came the day he encountered a skunk. Parthur was lying on his side, giving himself a grooming with his paws and tongue in a little meadow he had found near a thicket of blackberry bushes. He had just captured and eaten two small field mice and was feeling quite proud of himself. Suddenly, a large black and white skunk sauntered into his area. The skunk stopped when it saw Parthur but then it continued forward without much hesitation. Parthur could not believe the boldness of this animal. He could smell a strong pungent odor about the intruder and he jumped up and shook his head to clear his nose of the smell. Even after his encounters with the toad and the mole, Parthur decided maybe this animal was good to eat, in spite of the bad odor that seemed to surround it.

The skunk stopped moving when he spotted the young cat. He was in the middle of Parthur's little meadow now, only five feet away. Parthur began to circle the bold intruder, sizing him up for his next meal. The large black and white animal easily kept turning to face Parthur as the cat walked around and around the skunk. Parthur stopped circling and the skunk faced him with a cold blank stare from his round, black, bead-like eyes. The skunk, with its tail held high, stamped its feet several times as a warning to the young cat but Parthur took no heed and moved one small step closer to the skunk and stood still. The cat lowered his head and stared back at the impudent animal. Parthur had decided to attack this black and white striped animal but, before he could make his next move, the skunk twirled its body around and sprayed the unsuspecting cat straight in his face, with its awful musk.

Parthur was stricken. He momentarily couldn't see. The terrible smell was in his mouth, in his nose, in his eyes and all over his body. He rubbed his face in the grass trying to get some relief. He sneezed and coughed trying to get the stinking stuff out of his nose and mouth, as the skunk quickly and silently moved away from the area.

The cat was miserable. Finally, his vision started to return and he ran to the nearby river and rolled in the water and mud. Nothing seemed to help. For hours he tried to rub the smell off his body on trees, bushes, moss and leaves. He looked a mess and felt a mess. His fur was filled with mud, dirt, and pieces of grass and twigs he had picked up in his frenzy to rid himself of this terrible stench. It was days before he felt the smell was finally gone. That was one more animal he would avoid at all costs, from now on.

It was the middle of November and the days were becoming shorter and colder. Parthur's body had filled out well as he became fit and muscular, living and roaming free. He was over a year old now, and his fur was thick and shiny with a downy under coat. He had been on his own for several weeks and the feeling was exhilarating. Parthur had been following the Rock River east for many miles on his journey but now his instincts told him to head straight north. The houses were farther apart in this area and there were fewer roads to cross. Every day he was getting closer and closer to the Mississippi River and the Illiniwek Forest Preserve.

Chapter 30

Parthur passed numerous farms with big green fields of grazing cattle, pens of huge pigs, and even areas where the pigs had their own little houses. He slipped through acres of tall corn that rattled in the wind as their dry leaves rubbed up against each other and he crossed through many fields of swaying wheat that were great places for mouse hunts. Urgency had quickened his pace. Always, he was heading north, now.

One afternoon he came across a small farm nestled in a shallow valley that had a flock of white chickens. When Parthur spotted the farm as he walked out of some tangled underbrush on the top of a short hill, his first thought was to shy away from the area but just as he was about to turn away, the big rooster of the tiny flock crowed. Parthur stopped and looked down into the farmyard with interest where the chickens were pecking and scratching in the soft dirt. A light breeze was coming his way straight from those birds. Chickens, he smiled to himself. He sat down in the dry, brown grass on the top of the hill and stared down at the white, feathered group.

How could he nab one of those tasty birds? There was one big problem, however. As he watched the little flock with close interest, suddenly he was aware of a large, brown and white hound dog lying in the late afternoon sun on a patch of green-blue moss in the center of the barn yard. The dog had been sound asleep but now it was standing up and stretching itself. Parthur did not want to tangle with that dog but he sure wanted one of those chickens.

Parthur lay hidden on the small hilltop and watched. A heavy-set farmer in bib overalls appeared and Parthur watched him go about his chores from one small building to the next. The hound dog, now finished with his nap, chose to stay close to his master and padded slowly after him from chore to chore. Once, as the old farmer and his dog crossed the barnyard, the big dog stopped, sniffed the air and looked in Parthur's direction. The wind had shifted and now there was a slight breeze coming from Parthur's back. The hound bayed three times as he stared up at the hill where Parthur lay hidden. Parthur flattened himself to the ground, stiffened its body and was ready to bolt and run back into the forest but the dog soon lost interest and turned away. The dog followed the farmer into one of the barns. "What did you smell, Brownie?" the farmer asked the dog.

Parthur

"Was it a raccoon?" The farmer patted the dog's head then went about his chores.

Just after sunset, the farmer went into his house and Parthur was pleased to see the big dog went in with him. Parthur still waited. Quickly and quietly, night settled over the farm, but Parthur still waited. At times, a little speck of drool hung from his mouth as he anticipated the taste of one of those fat chickens and he would lick it away. Parthur knew exactly where all those chickens were. He had watched them patiently as they made their way into a small, wooden coop. Just before the farmer went into his house, the last thing he did was to close the door on his little flock.

Finally, all the color had left the late evening sky, and only the stars sparkled in the moonless, pitch black night. Parthur had his eyes fixed on the chicken coop as he carefully and slowly slid forward with his belly held low, his ears flattened to his head and each paw meeting the ground as soundlessly as a settling feather. The closer he got, the more the chickens' smell filled his nose as a light breeze now blew in the cat's direction. His stomach rumbled in anticipation of his next delicious meal. Fifty feet from the chicken coop, Parthur broke free of the tall grass and his cover and he dashed quickly and quietly those last few exposed feet to the door of the coop.

He stood motionless for a few seconds at the wooden barrier and listened. His cat's eyes searched through the dark of the night back to the farmer's house and he was certain the farmer and his dog did not know he was at the entrance of the chicken coop. Then he pawed at the old weathered door and was pleased to find that he could move it. It was held shut by an old, aging spring that would be of no match to an eager and hungry predator. It didn't take the young cat long before he had pulled it open far enough for him to squeeze inside.

There were about fifteen chickens in the coop, all sitting on long roosts on one side of the building. Parthur's scrapings at the coop door had not really alarmed them but he could tell they were getting a little restless as they shifted on their roosts and made soft clucking noises. He stood there quietly for a minute or two as he looked around the area. Their smell, plus the strong odor of their droppings, aroused the young cat as he stood poised on the floor of their home. Parthur gathered himself, and in one graceful jump he was on the roost grabbing a plump hen at the nape of her neck, killing her instantly.

Pandemonium broke loose. Chickens were everywhere, screeching and squawking. Their bodies banged into Parthur as he jumped down from the roost to the floor with the dead, white hen clamped securely in his mouth. The other chickens had gone into a frenzy. Their flapping bodies filled the air, and Parthur was having difficulty making his way back to the door of the coop. He crouched on the floor of the chicken coop with his prize in his mouth and waited for some of the bedlam to settle down. There came a short lull and then one of the chickens brushed up against him on the floor, and the panicked, shrill squawking started all over again.

Above all those sounds Parthur heard the dreaded barking and baying from that big hound dog. It sounded as if that dog was coming his way.

The farmer had heard his chickens raise the alarm as he was sitting at the kitchen table helping his high school son with his geometry. "Sounds like that pesky raccoon is back," he said, as he jumped up from the table. "Grab that big flashlight on the sink counter, son, and let's see if we can't get him tonight." The old hound dog was at the back door, frantically scratching at the bottom edge, eager for a chase.

"Hold on, Brownie." The farmer reached down and snapped a leash to his collar. "I don't want you racing into a situation you can't handle." He quickly handed the leash to his son and grabbed his Winchester double barrel shot gun propped up in a wooden gun rack next to the back door. A box of ammunition was on the shelf right above it, and the farmer fumbled quickly in the box and pulled out four red and brass shells.

As father, son and the dog raced out the kitchen door into the night, the farmer was shoving two of the shot gun shells into his gun and the other two into his pocket. His son, who was a skinny kid of fourteen, was being dragged by the hound towards the ruckus. The dog was pulling so hard on his leash he was choking himself while trying to gain each breath. The young boy was desperately trying to aim the beam of the flashlight in the direction of the chicken coop as they rushed out into the night but the dog was making that quite difficult.

Meanwhile, Parthur sensed the situation was getting dangerous. He pushed through the panicked chickens and made his way to the door. The door of the coop was open about six inches and Parthur used a paw to open it wider and forced his way through with the heavy bundle of the dead white hen. As he did, a rusty nail sliced into his shoulder. He winced with the pain of it but kept a tight grip on his prize and rushed out into the night. His pace was seriously hampered by the weight of the dead bird in his mouth but he couldn't bring himself to let go. So he rushed as fast as he could, straddling the limp white hen.

The farmer and his son with the baying dog pulling on his leash were only fifty feet away as Parthur leapt out the chicken, coop door. The son was frantically swinging the beam of the flashlight all around the barn yard. Then suddenly the light caught the fleeing cat with his prize clamped in his mouth. The young boy tried to steady the light squarely on him.

"It's a bobcat. It's a bobcat." the son screamed. "And he's got one of our chickens."

"Hold the light steady, son. I think I can get a good shot off," the father yelled over the baying of his dog. A horrendous sound ripped through the air and a large clump of dirt jumped up in front of Parthur.

"Damn, I missed him."

"Shoot again, Pa. Shoot again." the farmer's son screamed. The dog was going crazy. He was pulling so furiously on the leash the young boy found it almost impossible to hold the light on the fleeing cat but the bouncing beam gave the farmer one last glimpse of the running cat and his chicken and he shot again. The buckshot hit the dirt just to the side of Parthur with a mighty smack, throwing up dirt and rocks, missing the cat by only inches. The sound was deafening.

Parthur swerved from its impact. Quickly, the farmer leaned down and unhooked the leash from the dog's collar. "Go get him, Brownie," he yelled after the pursuing dog. The big hound dog needed no encouragement and he leaped in the direction of the fleeing cat.

Parthur didn't know if the farmer could shoot a third shot or not but he decided he had had enough, and it was time to get out of this area. He dropped the dead hen with regret and raced away into the night with the baying of the big hound dog close on his trail.

He took off north and ran as fast as he could. Parthur entered a heavily timbered area with thick underbrush that impeded him somewhat but the hound dog stuck with him. The hound wasn't getting any closer, in fact Parthur was pulling ahead of the dog but he wasn't losing him either. Parthur was beginning to panic. How could he get away from this animal? Most of the dogs Parthur had ever encountered had only chased him for a short distance and had then given up. This animal seemed intent on going forever.

Parthur ran into a grove of huge, tall oak trees, and without much hesitation, using his paws splayed wide to extend his claws and his strong hind legs to provide the boost, he scampered up one of the largest trees and sat in the crotch of a large limb and looked down. It didn't take long for the big brown and white hound dog to make it to the base of the tree where the cat sat.

The dog could not see him in the black of the night but he could smell the cat's scent where he had climbed up the trunk of the tree. The dog made several lunges as if trying to climb the tree himself, but he always slid down to its base. He circled around and around the tree, baying constantly. The dog was not going to leave this tree. He knew that cat was up there somewhere.

Parthur felt safe up in the tree but he needed to get away from that annoying animal. He climbed higher and higher in the tall oak tree. As he looked back in the direction of the farm and the chicken coop, he saw a faint light and heard the faraway voices of the farmer and his son making their way in his direction. As the hound dog kept up his incessant howling at the bottom of the tree, Parthur knew he had to make an escape somehow.

High up in the oak tree where Parthur was crouched, he realized the tree he was in was pushed up against another large oak tree right next to him. He could see another large limb on the neighboring tree he thought he could reach. He crouched low on the branch he was sitting on and with his haunches raised high, made a quick jump and landed in the other tree. He lost his balance for just a second but quickly, his claws caught hold of the new limb and he righted himself. He had made little noise with the switch of trees. He looked down. The big dog had not noticed he had changed trees. The hound was too intent on the cat's scent on the trunk of the tree that he was guarding. He bayed continuously as he looked up into 'his' tree.

Parthur was able to change trees eight more times. Each time he landed in a new tree farther away, he checked back to see if the dog had left the base of the tree he had climbed originally. He had not. Parthur was now seventy feet away from the dog and the original oak tree he had climbed.

Carefully and quietly, he inched his way down backwards on the back side of the trunk of that last tree. When he hit the ground, he stood quietly for a few seconds. Then he peered from behind the tree to see what the hound was doing. Sure enough, the dog had not moved his position. He was still howling and baying at what he thought was the prize. Just then, the farmer and his son made it to the dog's side.

"Is he up there, Brownie?" The farmer's son searched the branches of the big oak tree with the large flashlight beam. "I don't see anything."

Parthur knew he needed to leave the grove of trees as fast as he could. Noiselessly he raced off into the darkness of the night and faded into the woods.

Parthur ran for another thirty minutes without stopping. He was exhausted. He stopped by a little stream to get a quick drink. His shoulder hurt where the nail had pierced him. He licked the inch-long wound carefully to make certain it was clean. He would be a little stiff for a while but, other than that, he was fine. Way off in the distance, he could still hear that old hound dog. He wasn't getting any closer now. Parthur hoped the dog and his owners would not figure out what had happened and just tire of the chase. Parthur moved on north.

It was almost daybreak and Parthur had not been able to hear the baying sounds of the dog for hours. He was tired and hungry. Accidently, he found a small cave in among some rocks. He went in and out of the small enclosure several times. He liked the feel of it. He went back in, checked and cleaned his wounded shoulder one more time and collapsed into a fitful sleep, deep within its protection. Food would have to wait. Right now, he needed rest.

In his flight from the farmer's hound dog, Parthur had still been guided by his inner compass to head north. He had run deep into the Illiniwek Forest Preserve. The Mississippi River lay just over the hill from the little cave the animal had found.

By evening time, Parthur, refreshed from his long rest, roused himself and ventured out of his little alcove. He looked around this new area. The place felt good to him, and he felt no need to travel any further. He found a small creek nearby and he refreshed himself. He picked up the scent of rabbits and saw a small mouse scurry into its hole. He circled the area several times. He trotted to the top of a nearby hill and looked off into the distance and saw the big, wide river below him. He remembered river from his stay at the Fritz's home. He lifted his head, closed his eyes and took in its smells from the soft breeze that was wafting up the hill toward him. His nostrils quivered from the memory of it.

The cat went back to the entrance of the cave and made his decision. This would be home; he would travel no more. He let out a low, throaty yowl to celebrate his arrival that reverberated among the trees. A lone crow that had been watching him was flushed from his perch with the sound and flew off to the west. Parthur watched him fly away and then went off in search of a meal.

It was late December when he experienced his first snowfall. Parthur's fur had become long and thick with the changing seasons and he had long, gleaming guard hairs that were individually pigmented with bands of pale gold and gray that covered his soft under fur*. He had a creamy white bib of hair that was flecked with black that hung from his chest. All of it was waterproofed so, as he stepped out of his cave into the soft falling white stuff, he didn't feel the cold. When the small flakes hit his nose, he swatted at them as if they were insects. The swirling cold flakes excited him, and he pranced as he tasted and felt it. He stopped and flicked his feet to rid his paws of the stuff. He stuck his nose into a small drift of snow and felt the chill of it and sneezed. He could see his breath in the brisk air and he did another little dance then rolled over and over in the soft drifts to experience the touch and feel of it again.

As Parthur played in the snow, he moved quite a distance from his cave. Suddenly, he jumped to his feet. He sniffed the air and then the ground. He saw paw prints in the snow leading away from his area up a nearby valley. He followed the sight and scent of these prints for over a quarter of a mile. He stopped for a while and pondered this new development. He had never smelled this smell before. A shiver went through him. He now knew he was not the only one of his kind in these woods. He put his nose in the air and sniffed in the direction of the fading footprints and then turned and headed back to his den

Parthur

Chapter 31

Bobcats are usually an independent breed of animal. The males, once they leave their mothers, usually spend their entire life on their own. The only time they seek out the company of other bobcats is in the spring at mating time. Parthur, however, had spent so much time in the company of humans; he had become a social animal. He was curious about the tracks he had seen in the snow that winter but he waited patiently until late February before he decided it was time to investigate his neighbor.

Parthur headed south of his den in his quest. Bobcats mark their territories by spraying urine, leaving fecal mounds or clawing on tree trunks. Ten miles south, he crossed into the territory of an old male bobcat. When Parthur smelled his scent markings liberally scattered throughout the old cat's area, he immediately turned and headed into a more easterly direction then he found her area, the smell he remembered from early last winter. He knew its owner by the scat piles and urine scents she had left to mark her space.

Parthur stopped and considered what he wanted to do next. It was not mating season, yet. Would the female prefer to be left on her own? What would she think of a curious young male coming for a social visit? He lifted and twitched his nose in the air, trying to sense where she might be. He paused for some time then he made his decision. He had come this far and he was going to try to find her.

He spent hours searching for her. This was definitely her area but where was she? It wasn't until the next day he discovered her on a small ledge in a large rock pile where her spotted coat appeared to merge with the sun-dappled stones around her. She was having an afternoon snooze in the little sunlight left on that cool late February day on a flat stone that had retained the heat of the over-head sun. Parthur watched her for a while from his hiding place in the thick, dry grasses that formed big clumps among small dirty snow patches that still had not melted from winter's bounty. Bare trees reached up and out all around him. He watched as a light breeze moved the fur of her mutton chops. He noticed her paws and tail twitching in her sleep as she dreamed. Finally, he just couldn't help himself. He stood up in full view and let out a small mournful cry of introduction.

The young female bolted out of her sleep, stood up and came to attention. She looked in the direction of Parthur and fixed him with a cold, uninviting stare. Parthur called to her again and moved a few feet closer and sat down. She never moved, except for her short tail that was switching back and forth. Parthur stood up and moved closer. Once again, he sat down. He was now just below her rock ledge and he started to give himself a complete bath while feigning dis-interest in her the whole time. Rhythmically, he dragged his rough tongue down one shoulder and across his back and then repeated it on the other shoulder. He did it again and again but he carefully took note of her with each lift of his head. Then he gave a large, tongue curling yawn as if he really wasn't interested. She watched him with close attention. She gave a lip curling hiss then she began to move.

Who was this intruder? How dare he come into her area, call to her and then just ignore her. This strange feline was failing to comply with bobcat etiquette but her curiosity got the best of her and she just had to get closer. Slowly, she inched her way off the ledge. She stopped every few feet and sat; never taking her eyes off him. Each time she would stare at her visitor, lift her nose and breathe in his scent. Then she would move closer. Meanwhile, Parthur watched her carefully out of the corner of his eye as he finished his cleaning.

Finally, only three feet separated the two animals. She sat in front of him and the two animals stared at each other. Periodically, they would stretch out their necks, squint their eyes and sniff through flared nostrils toward each other. It was Parthur who made the first move to make contact. He stood up and moved toward her. The young female jumped back a few feet. His size was a little intimidating to her. Parthur stopped and stood still watching her. When she sensed he meant no harm, she turned back toward him, took a few steps in his direction and stared long and hard at him again. She stood her ground on tensed legs, ready to flee at a moment's notice.

Parthur slowly walked toward her and touched her nose. She flinched back just a little with the contact but then she reached out her nose and they touched again. They stood there for a few moments and then rubbed cheeks. She got up and circled Parthur carefully, as he stood quietly in place. His head swiveled as he watched her walk around him. Then she was back in front of him and they touched cheeks again. Parthur reached out and butted her head with his. She butted back. They had accepted each other.

The young female was a little younger than Parthur. She had not borne any kittens yet and she probably would not for another year. She had left her mother only a few months before and was just getting used to being on her own. There were times she missed being with others of her own kind. She had been one of two kittens that her mother had delivered last spring. Her sister had gone her own way. So, when this friendly male showed up, she was happy for the company.

The two of them spent three days together. They played together, they hunted together, they groomed each other and they spent afternoon naps together but finally, Parthur felt the urge to leave her. He needed to go back to his area. He knew, however, that he would see her again.

Parthur

Chapter 32

It was June before Parthur finally decided it was time to go back and find the young female that lived southeast of his den. He entered her area early one afternoon and spent several hours carefully seeking out her whereabouts. This time, he found her sitting next to a small creek where she was idly watching small minnows darting in and out among the rocks. He was much bolder about presenting himself to her at this meeting. He was only twenty feet away when he called to her with a soft breeze at his back. He sat down and waiting to see her response.

Upon hearing his call, she sprang to attention, arched her back and hissed. She lifted her nose into the air and breathed in his scent. Parthur did not move. She knew this young male and calmed immediately. She sat back down and watched him carefully. Parthur waited only a few moments but when he was sure she recognized him and would accept him again, he slowly moved toward her. When he reached her, they touched noses and butted heads. She was glad to see Parthur and he was happy to be with her.

The young female did enjoy the company of this big male bobcat. They stayed by the little creek until dark, grooming one another and just snoozing side by side. A large moon was just breaking over the treetops when the two young bobcats left the little creek in search of food but, before the hunt began, they went off on a crazy zigzag run with each other. It was a game of tag among the trees and underbrush of the woods. First, he led and she chased after him. Sensing he was much faster than the young female, Parthur slowed down so she could catch up. She batted at his hind quarters and then darted ahead of him. He chased after her, catching up with her easily. He ran alongside of her for a while then he batted at her hind quarters and sped past. For over twenty minutes they played their special made-up game, dancing in the splotches of moonlight that touched the floor of the thick woods. Then suddenly, the two running animals broke through a small clearing. In front of them stood the dark silhouette of a large log cabin home.

Both cats stopped abruptly. The female turned and quickly slunk back behind a nearby bush but Parthur stood and stared at the familiar house. He knew this place. This was where Dawn had lived. He lifted his nose into the light breeze that was coming from the direction of the house. He could smell Ken's dogs, and he almost turned and left the area but he remembered Dawn and the other two people who lived here. Parthur stood there and pondered his discovery. This must be why he was drawn to this area.

The young female was quite confused by Parthur's reaction to this place that housed people and dogs. She too could smell their odors and she wanted to leave this area immediately. She hissed and called quietly to Parthur but he didn't move. He looked over his shoulder at her and then stared back at the house. She waited patiently behind him but had chosen the safety of the thick brush, ready to run at the first sign of danger.

Then she saw Parthur sit down, showing no inclination to leave. She slowly crept out from behind her hiding place. Her heart was pounding with fear but she carefully approached him. He didn't seem to notice her so she batted at his hind quarters with her front paw. He turned to her and let out a low growl. Confused, she retreated to the safety of the brush again and watched as Parthur remained there out in the open, staring at that house. She sat down and waited as he pondered the big, dark building in the night.

Then, suddenly, she watched in horror as Parthur stood up and walked resolutely toward the house. She moved among the bushes to get a better view of what he was doing but she lost sight of him as he got closer to the building. She was pretty certain she heard him climb a large oak tree that was quite near the log structure. What was he doing? She slunk back into the underbrush where she watched, waited and listened.

Suddenly, the night's silence was broken by one low, mournful, call from Parthur. He was calling to the house. What could he be thinking? The young female bobcat wondered but she didn't move. There was a long silence then he called one more time.

About five minutes after Parthur's last call, both cats listened as they heard the back-screen door open on the little porch at the back of the house. The female bobcat was crouched and ready to flee. The figure of a lone man appeared and stood there in the moonlight. He hesitated for a few minutes but when Parthur didn't offer another serenade, he slowly went back into the dark house.

It wasn't long before the young female saw Parthur trotting back to where he had last seen her. She stepped out of her hiding place as he approached her. She batted at his front legs and made a small growl but Parthur ignored her. He moved past her into the underbrush and she followed. She couldn't believe what he had just done. The two of them slunk off into the velvet night.

Chapter 33

It was spring in Yuma, and I was finishing up my second year of teaching at Kofa High School. The new school had its first senior class to graduate from Kofa, the class of 1962. Because this initial graduation was considered a big deal at the school, all faculty were in attendance for the momentous day. As I sat in the bleachers of the gymnasium, watching the seniors march by in their graduation caps and gowns, I thought back over my two years of teaching there in Yuma. It really had been a great time. I loved the school, the students and my friends.

My principal, Mr. Armstrong, had offered me a contract to teach at Kofa High School for the next year but I wasn't sure I was going to come back. Two months earlier, I had applied for an overseas teaching position with the United States Air Force. I had interviewed two weeks earlier in San Diego but I had not heard anything from them yet. I was intrigued with the idea of teaching American students in a foreign country. I really loved it here at Kofa High but something was tugging at me to spread my wings and see the world.

Mr. Armstrong understood. "Dawn, we would love to have you come back here. If you decide against the overseas teaching job, let me know. There will always be a place here for you."

The graduation ceremony was finally over and I said my good-byes to all my teaching buddies with hugs and promises to keep in touch. I reached the parking lot and was about to get into my car when I heard, "Miss Fritz. Oh, Miss Fritz. Wait a minute." I turned and saw Amy Stanton breathlessly running toward me. Amy was clutching her graduation cap to her head as she rushed up to me and gave me a big hug. "I am so glad I caught you before you left," she said enthusiastically. "Thank you for everything. You really have been an inspiration to me. Did I tell you I was accepted at the University of Arizona?"

"No, Amy, I didn't know. That is great."

"I'm going to become a teacher just like you."

"Amy, I am touched. You will be a good one, I am sure." I took Amy's hand, "And, Amy, thanks again for Mully. I really do love him. He is a darling cat. That was very thoughtful of you. I will never forget your kindness."

Amy beamed then turned, "Well, goodbye, Miss Fritz. You were always my favorite teacher." She rushed off to be with her family, who were waiting patiently at their car. I watched her go, smiled, waved to her family who waved back and then got into my little car and drove out of the Kofa High School's parking lot for the last time. I thought back to the night Amy was in the school's station wagon in Gila Bend; the night I had picked up the bobcat kitten, Parthur. I shook my head. I was not going to revisit that painful memory.

I planned on leaving Yuma for Illinois early the next morning. After the graduation ceremony, I rushed back to my apartment and spent the rest of the day packing up my car. I spent a restless night and was wide awake at 5:30. I showered quickly and tried to be as quiet as I could because of my roommate, Berle, but in spite of my care, Berle and her little dog, Twitch, stumbled sleepily out of their room around 6 o'clock.

"We're sure going to miss you, Dawn," she said.

"Me, too." I was packing up my last few items from the bathroom.

I filled my arms with these last pieces of my belongings and headed out of the apartment door.

"I'll be back for Mully," I said over my shoulder to Berle. I tucked these last few items into my already packed car and returned to the apartment. "Well, Berle, I guess this is it." I hugged my good friend, and both of us had tears in our eyes. Mully, my cat, had been sitting on the couch. I walked over, picked him up and headed for the door.

"You will keep in touch?" Berle asked.

"Of course."

"I'll be anxious to hear if you hear from that overseas teaching job."

"I'm still not sure if I will take it even if they do offer it to me."

"Do let me know. Twitch and I would love to be your roommates again next year."

"You will be the first to know." I smiled and walked out of the apartment, carrying Mully in my arms.

Berle put on her fluffy pink bath robe, picked up Twitch, and followed me out of the apartment to my car. She stopped at the end of the breezeway and watched as I carefully added Mully to the fully loaded car. I slid into the front seat and closed the door. I rolled down the driver's side window. "Goodbye, Berle," I called out the window, and waved as I backed out of the apartment parking lot.

"Goodbye," Berle yelled back. "Don't forget to keep in touch." She cuddled her little dog in her left arm and waved with her free hand.

"I will," I answered and I waved again. I straightened out my little car and headed east for the interstate. I would miss the two of them, Berle and Twitch, especially if I was off to Europe the next fall.

I had several friends I planned to visit on my way back to the Midwest, so it was mid-June by the time I drove up the long gravel driveway of Hawthorn Hill to my parent's home in Illinois. My parents were pleased to have me back home again for the summer and they loved the black fluffy cat I had brought home.

When we all sat down to dinner that first night, I reflexively looked under the dinner table for Parthur. That's where he would have been last summer. I quickly looked up when I realized what I had done but my father read the hurt look on my face.

Parthur

"We all miss him, Dawn," he said softly.

No one had spoken of Parthur since I had returned home but I just couldn't stop all the memories. I swallowed hard to remove the large lump in my throat.

"You know, I heard something last night," Ken went on. "I'm not quite sure what to make of it."

"What did you hear?" I asked.

"If I hear it again tonight, I'll wake you."

I thought that was rather strange. What sound could he have heard that would make him want to wake me in the middle of the night? I didn't have the opportunity to question my father any more about the strange sound he had heard because the phone rang. It was for me. My best friend from high school, Vera, was calling. We talked and laughed over old times, set a date to get together the following Saturday night then I returned to the dinner table. "I'm sorry, Mom, I should have called her back and not taken the call during dinner." Mother and Father were finishing their meals. I pushed my half-eaten plate away. I really didn't feel much like eating anyway.

"That's all right, Dawn," my mom started clearing the table. My father said nothing more about the strange sound he had heard the night before and I didn't think to bring it up again. Mom served dessert.

I watched a little TV with my folks but when the 10 o'clock news came on, I said my goodnights and was the first to head off to bed. I had been driving all day and was exhausted. I picked up Mully and headed to my childhood bedroom and bed. The two of us fell asleep almost immediately on that first night back on Hawthorn Hill.

Parthur

CHAPTER 34

It must have been close to 2 o'clock in the morning when I felt a soft shake on my shoulder. "Dawn. Dawn, wake up," my dad whispered close to my ear.

I struggled out of a deep sleep and looked up at my dad. "What's up?"

He quickly put his finger to his lips. By the light of a bright moon outside my bedroom window I could see my father's face indicating I should be quiet.

"Come with me," he said softly as he turned and started to leave my room.

I jumped out of bed and threw on my housecoat as I quickly came awake. My dad was waiting just outside of my bedroom and I followed him through the dark house into the kitchen. I certainly was curious why he had awakened me in the middle of the night. He carefully opened the screen door that led out of the kitchen onto the back porch. He silently beckoned me to follow him and I walked out behind him as he held the door. I watched as he gently closed the screen door so that it made no sound. The two of us stood on the small, square, wooden porch bathed in the bright moonlight. I turned to my dad with a questioning look on my face. He leaned in close to me and whispered in my ear, "Just listen."

I moved closer to the wooden banister and listened to the night sounds as I peered off into the woods that bordered the back yard of my parents' home. The katydids, the crickets and all other types of night insects were singing their own personal songs of the night. I closed my eyes as I listened to them as they brought back so many memories of my childhood growing up here on Hawthorn Hill. Then I heard the sound of a lone whippoorwill making his call down by the back ravine. I smiled. I always liked the mournful call of that bird. It always reminded me of home. I opened my eyes and looked at my dad expectantly but he just shook his head and pointed to his ears.

"Listen," he mouthed to me again.

We stood there for a few minutes longer, both of us looking off into the dark. What could my dad possibly want me to hear out here? Then it happened. The night air was broken by a low, mournful cat sound, a wild cat, and it was in a tree that was only thirty feet away from the little porch we stood on. I froze. The sound was eerie and hypnotic in the moonlight, almost as a woman's scream but lower. It wasn't a distress call but the animal that was making the sound seemed as if it were calling for someone. Instinctively, I knew it was a bobcat's call. Quickly, I turned to the direction of the call and I impulsively cried out, "Parthur." Then I hesitated. "Parthur, is that you?" There was a long silence. Then the night's stillness was broken again with the piercing and mournful call as the mysterious animal answered me. It made prickles run up and down my arms.

Could it be? Hope lighted my face as I turned to my father and excitedly whispered, "Dad, that has to be Parthur." I turned again to face the area where I had last heard the bobcat and called, "Parthur. Parthur." Once again there was an answer. There was a slight rustle in the tree from which his calls had been coming. My father and I heard the animal leave its perch and scamper down the trunk of the tree, his claws scraping on the bark. We both waited. We could scarcely breathe, not knowing what to expect. Might he scamper up the back steps? Would he show himself in the back yard? We waited for a good fifteen minutes. Several times I called his name again, but there were no more responses. The animal was gone.

"Dad, I can't believe it. It has to be Parthur." The two of us remained on the porch for several more minutes, searching the dark night for any sight of the mysterious visitor.

My dad touched my arm. "Let's go inside. Whatever it was or whoever it was, it is gone now."

The two of us turned to return to the kitchen. I looked back over my shoulder as we left the porch.

My mom had been standing just inside the screen door and had heard everything. She switched on the kitchen light. "Mom, did you hear that? I know it's Parthur."

"I heard it."

"Dawn, the ranger said he died," my dad softly added.

"I don't care what he said. That is my bobcat. It was Parthur. I know it is."

"But there are other bobcats in our woods. It could have been a wild bobcat," my mom added.

"No way." I answered emphatically. "No wild bobcat would ever have come that close to our house. He was calling for us." Then I thought for a few moments, "He answered me, Dad. He really did. You heard him."

"Dawn, don't get your hopes up."

"Dad, he's alive. Parthur is alive. I don't know how but he's alive." I pondered over what we had just experienced. "Dad, is that what you heard the night before I got home? Did a bobcat call to the house that night?"

"Yes, I did hear something very much like tonight." He hesitated a bit. "Maybe you had better go visit Jeff Long at the wild animal farm tomorrow. He might be able to shed some light on our mysterious visitor."

The three of us sat at the kitchen table for some time, discussing the possibility Parthur was really alive and he had found us. But how? Finally, we all left the kitchen and headed to our bedrooms, but I was so excited about the mysterious wildcat visit and his calls I could hardly get back to sleep that night. *It just has to be Parthur*, I kept telling myself as I slowly fell into a fitful sleep. Morning just couldn't come fast enough.

Chapter 35

Bright and early the next morning I was out of the house and heading to the wild animal farm in Moline. I pulled up in front of the ranger house a few minutes before seven thirty. Jeff and Barbara were just finishing their breakfast when I rapped on their door.

"Dawn." Jeff exclaimed. "What a great surprise. Come on in. What brings you all the way in here this early in the morning?"

I didn't move from the doorstep. "Jeff, you are not going to believe this but a wild cat came to our house last night. He was really close, Jeff. He called to me, I answered him and then he answered me." I went on and on and told all the details of the previous night's visit as quickly as I could. Barbara joined Jeff at the opened door and listened intently to my story. "Jeff, what can you tell me?" I looked from Jeff to Barbara and then back to Jeff again. "Did Parthur really die?"

Jeff looked at Barbara. She gave a slight nod. He sighed and then said, "Dawn, he got real sick." He stopped and looked at Barbara again. She smiled and gave another little nod of her head. "Well, when he got so sick, we brought him into the ranger house to see if we could nurse him back to health." He hesitated again, "Dawn, he got away from us here. One morning he dashed out our back door and jumped over..."

I never let him finish. "Jeff, he is alive. I knew it. I knew it." I was off their doorstep, and I rushed to my car. "Oh, thank you. Thank you," I called over my shoulder.

Jeff stood at the door and called after me, "Dawn, if it is Parthur, remember he is now a full-grown, wild bobcat. Be careful. He could be dangerous." He wanted to explain more to her. He wanted to tell Dawn why he had said the bobcat was dead and how he had been certain it could never have made it on its own. He wanted to explain how he had not wanted to put Dawn and her family through that anguish but she was in her car, waving to him as she drove down his driveway before he could say any more. As he walked back into the kitchen, Jeff said to his wife, "I hope she's right. I hope it is Parthur. I'd like to think he made it."

"Do you think she will try and make contact with him?" his wife asked.

"Knowing Dawn, I'm sure she will."

"Wouldn't that be dangerous?"

"It could be. She did raise him from a kitten. If it is her pet, he must have some memories of all that, otherwise, why would he come back to their place but how could he have found their home? It's almost thirty miles from here." He hesitated as he thought about that. "I will call her once I am sure she is back home."

I rushed back to Hawthorn Hill to tell my parents the extraordinary news. They were just finishing their breakfast as I rushed up the back stairs and into the kitchen. "Dad. Mom. It has to be Parthur. He got away from Jeff and now he has come back to his home here at Hawthorn Hill." I quickly related what Jeff had said.

"Whoa, slow down. You can't be sure," my dad said. "Do you know how many miles he would have had to cover to just get here from the wild animal farm? Do you have any idea how many major roads he would have had to cross, or how many neighborhoods he would have had to get through?"

"I don't care. I just know it is him. I am absolutely certain."

At that moment, the phone rang. My mom answered it. "Dawn, it is for you."

I gave my mother a questioning look and she shrugged her shoulders, indicating she didn't know who it was. I took the phone.

"Is this Dawn Fritz?"

"Yes."

"This is Harry Montgomery. I work for the Dependent Schools in Europe for the Air Force."

"Yes?"

"Dawn, we have carefully gone over your credentials and records as a teacher, we liked your interview and now we would like to offer you a job teaching English in one of our Junior High Schools in France this fall. Would you be interested?"

I paused for just a second and a huge smile covered my face. It didn't take me long to say yes. "Yes, I really would be interested."

"Great," Harry Montgomery answered. "We will be putting the offer in the mail today but I will go over some of the details with you." Harry and I talked for the next twenty minutes. I keep asking questions, and he filled me in on all the information.

When I finally hung up, I was ecstatic. "I got the job in Europe," I told my mom, who had just finished the breakfast dishes and was now preparing a soup for lunch while I had been talking on the kitchen phone.

"That's wonderful," my mom said. She dried her hands on her apron and gave me a big hug. "So, you really are going to do it?"

I hesitated for only a moment. "Yes," I said, "I really want to do this." I was so excited about my new job. France. Wow, my mind was racing. I quickly told my mom the details Harry Montgomery and I had discussed on the phone. Harry had told me I would be teaching at a Junior High School for American students at Laon Air Base, which was situated just outside of the city of Laon, France. I would be about an hour and a half north of Paris and an hour and a half south of Brussels. I had never been to France, let alone Europe, and the thought of all the beautiful pictures I had ever seen of that majestic city, Paris. "France," I whispered to myself, again.

Parthur

Then there was the prospect of Parthur. Was he really out there? Would the mystery cat return tonight so I could be certain if it truly was him? I was so excited about that possibility. My mind was in a whirlwind.

Jeff Long from the wild animal farm called me soon after the phone call about my new job. He tried to explain why he had told my father Parthur was dead. "I just didn't want you to worry. I didn't think there was any way he could make it."

"It's OK, Jeff. I understand."

"Dawn, it might not be Parthur."

"He answered me, Jeff. I know it's him."

"You aren't going to try and make contact with him, are you?" Jeff asked. "If it is Parthur, he has been on his own for over a year. Dawn, it could be dangerous."

"Don't worry, Jeff." At that point I didn't know what I planned to do. "But I will be careful," I ended the conversation with the ranger.

All day I watched the clock as its hands just seemed to creep around the dial. Would the mystery cat come back that night? My parents and I talked about my new job in Europe. I could hardly believe I was really and truly going to Europe next fall to teach. My head was in a spin. I needed to call Mr. Armstrong, the principal of Kofa High back in Yuma. I didn't want him to hold a teaching spot for me. I could hardly wait to get the paperwork from the Dependent Schools of Europe. There were so many questions and details I still needed answered but what a thrill next fall would be. *Then, was Parthur out there? Would he come back tonight?*

Not much was said about Parthur between my parents and me for the rest of the day. The big news was my European job but in the back of all our minds, all three of us were wondering if the mystery cat would truly come back for another visit. I tried to listen to my mom and dad's conversations around the dinner table that night but I didn't add much to their chit chat. So much had happened this day. I just wanted the night to come.

At twilight, I was on the big wrap-around porch, pacing back and forth. My dad sat down in a large wicker chair in the dim light and watched me. "Dawn, he might not even come back tonight," he reasoned.

"He'll be here," was all I could say.

Chapter 36

As darkness fell over Hawthorn Hill, I pulled a long wicker chaise on the screened porch over to the area that overlooked the backyard where I had heard the bobcat the night before. I sat down and propped my head up on the back of the chaise. It squeaked and crackled as I got into position. I had a light blanket, and I tucked it in around myself against the cool breeze that was coming off the Mississippi River behind me. Summer nights on Hawthorn Hill were always pleasant. I breathed in the familiar smells. I waited and I listened.

I loved the nights at Hawthorn Hill. The sounds of the night were so soothing and musical. There was a large, almost-full moon rising above the horizon and the whole hill was bathed in its soft silver light. The insects were singing their magical night songs that ebbed and flowed over me as I sat huddled on the couch, waiting. Hours went by, and I heard nothing. I was getting concerned. Would he come back? In spite of my will to stay awake, I was drawn into a soft sleep by the sounds all around me. Hours passed.

Suddenly, the nighttime serenade changed. There was something out there that caused the other voices to hush and listen. I came out of my light sleep, and in an instant threw off the light blanket and listened as well. Sure enough, there it was again. The bobcat was back. His low, mournful, throaty yowl filled the air.

I jumped to my feet and was at the back-screen door about to open it when my father intercepted me. He had been waiting and listening, too. "Are you sure you want to go out there? That's a wild animal. If it is Parthur, he's been on his own for some time." He took hold of my arm. "He could have changed. There could be danger."

"I have to do this, Dad." I stepped away from my father out to the back porch. "I'll be careful." I really hadn't thought about what I would do if the mystery cat came back but, when I heard that call, I knew I had to try and make contact.

My dad stepped out on the back porch and watched me. I almost flew down the back steps and walked resolutely to the area where I had last heard the sounds of the animal. I was standing at the rear of the yard, which backed up onto the woods to the south of the property. The moon was high in the sky now and the whole area was washed with its soft, blue-white light. I turned toward the woods and called softly, "Parthur? Parthur, it's me." The trees and bushes swayed as a soft breeze moved through the area, but I heard no response. "Parthur?" I called again.

Then I heard a soft rustle in the underbrush just ten feet in front of me. I waited breathlessly. I could feel my heart pounding in my chest. My whole body was tense with anticipation. "Parthur?" I called softly again. Then slowly, the tall grass parted and standing in front of me was a full grown, large adult bobcat. I stooped down slowly into a crouched position and held out my hand to him. "Parthur, it's me," I whispered again, almost afraid to speak for fear he would dash back into the dark.

The large bobcat stared hard at the young woman in front of him. He stood motionless except for a slight swish of his short tail. He raised his head, cocked his ears and sniffed the air as he eyed the familiar form.

I dropped to my knees and remained very still with my hand outstretched, and then a thought came to me. I slowly raised my thumb and gave the 'thumbs up' sign.

Parthur looked at me, hesitated then slowly picked up his front paw and tapped pat, pat, pat.

"Parthur, it's really you," I whispered, as tears filled my eyes.

Slowly and tentatively the bobcat moved toward me until his nose was just a foot away from my outstretched hand.

I could see his nostrils as they wrinkled back and forth pulling in my scent. "Parthur, it's me." I now sat down on the ground still holding out my hand for the animal to smell.

The sound of Dawn's voice washed over the animal and brought back all the memories of her when he was a kitten and growing up. Was this the person who was the only mother he could remember? He moved forward a few more inches and breathed in the smell of her hand as he closed his eyes and remembered. Then, suddenly and abruptly, he knew it was her and he rushed forward those last few inches and pushed up against her with a loving rub and a butt to her shoulders.

Tears were streaming down my cheeks as I grabbed hold of his head and shoulders in a big bear hug. "Oh, Parthur, it's really, really you," I sobbed. I buried my face into his soft fur and pulled him close to my chest. Parthur began to lick my arms, hands and finally my face. He couldn't seem to get close enough and kept pushing up against me. I stroked his back and head as he stretched in pleasure at my touch. I even found that special spot behind his right ear, and I gave it a good scratching. He closed his eyes with the pleasure and the memory of it.

His body felt so different to me now. I could feel the strong, developed muscles under his soft fur. He wasn't a baby anymore. He was a strong, big and beautiful animal. I felt the raised scar on his shoulder from his night in the chicken coop and I wondered what might have caused this healed over wound.

We sat there together, enjoying the closeness of each other. When I would stop stroking his body, Parthur would nudge my arm and hand with his wet nose telling me to keep it up. Periodically, he reached over and washed my face with several swipes of his sandpaper tongue.

Then, suddenly, I heard a soft rustle in the grass twenty feet away. Parthur stiffened in my arms, and we both looked in that direction. I could just barely make out what was there. In the soft shadows I could see the dim outline of another bobcat, as it moved slowly from bush to bush. Parthur, staring at the silent shadow, made a low rumbling sound in his throat that sounded like a greeting. There was a soft rumbling sound back from the bushes as the other bobcat answered. I understood, "Oh, Parthur, you have a mate."

Parthur pulled away from me and stood a few feet away looking in the direction of the other cat. He glanced back at me then he looked out into the darkness again. "Go," I whispered. "Go and be happy." Parthur looked back at me one more time. He hesitated then he bounded off into the shadows of the night.

I sat at our meeting place for some time, hugging my knees in the pale, soft moonlight. I didn't want to leave this magical site that had brought us back together again. That beautiful, wonderful night was blurred by the tears that flooded my eyes and rolled down my cheeks yet I was so happy. He had made it. He was free. It was as it should be.

Notes

*Rydon, Hope. 1990. Bobcat year. Lyons & Burford, New York, NY.

**Photo courtesy of the *Moline Daily Dispatch*

About the Author

Dawn Fritz Hopkins

This story is based on the true story as experienced by the author, Dawn Fritz Hopkins. She graduated from the University of New Mexico in the spring of 1960. That fall she took a teaching job at Kofa High School in Yuma, Arizona, where she acquired Parthur. She taught there for two years and then took a teaching position with the United States Air Force at Laon Air Force Base, Laon, France.

After one year in France, she moved to Germany and taught for one year at Sembach Air Force Base and three years at Ramstein Air Force Base. It was in Germany that she met her future husband, Edward (Ted) Hopkins, a fighter pilot in the Air Force. They were married in 1965 in the Air Force Chapel at Sembach, Germany.

Her husband left the Air Force in 1967 to pursue a business career, and they returned to America to raise a family of three children, Mark, Scott and Paige. In the course of her husband's career, they lived in Ohio, Illinois, Missouri, Indiana, Pennsylvania, Wisconsin and Arizona. His work allowed them to travel much of the world. Their favorite place, however, is London.

Dawn is a calligrapher and has taught hundreds of students this beautiful art form. She also formed the Sonoran Speakers Club in Scottsdale, Arizona, and ran it for eleven seasons bringing speakers from all over the world to her audiences.

Dawn and Ted are now retired and live in Edmond, Oklahoma.

Made in the USA
Lexington, KY
19 December 2019